About the author

Michelle Burgess began to write as a way to entertain her grandchildren. The lead characters in this book, are largely inspired by her own children and grandchildren and her love of the natural world and all things magical and mysterious. What began as a bedtime story turned into the first instalment in the series *Widdershins*.

THE BOOK OF WIDDERSHINS

Michelle Burgess

THE BOOK OF WIDDERSHINS

Vanguard Press

VANGUARD PAPERBACK

© Copyright 2020
Michelle Burgess

A CIP catalogue record for this title is
available from the British Library.

ISBN 9781784657-42 0

Vanguard Press is an imprint of
Pegasus Elliot MacKenzie Publishers Ltd.
www.pegasuspublishers.com

First Published in 2020

Vanguard Press
Sheraton House Castle Park
Cambridge England

Printed & Bound in Great Britain

Dedication

This book, my first book, is dedicated to those that inspired me both then and now as they lit a fire in my heart and my imagination that will burn brightly for them every day. My beautiful daughters, Kairen, Shiona and Jessica, my life was complete with the power of three. My wonderful grandchildren, Roison, Mark and Elliott. My own mother once said, "I didn't think it was possible to love any child that you hadn't given birth to as much as this," when speaking of her own grandchildren. Now I am blessed by being a grandmother myself, I understand the depth of love she was referring to.

My wonderful mother, who is my biggest fan and my favourite critic; if I turn out to be half the woman she is, my life will be a success.

Life without love is cold and a life without imagination is a baron land. I am truly blessed to live in the warmth of a beautiful garden.

Chapter One
Roisin

"No! Roisin, don't go through!" Mark called after his sister, He wasn't sure if she heard him.

Just as she disappeared into the eerie fog, he saw her turn around and reach out her hand. "Mark," she called as she looked back over her shoulder. Her voice was so feint it was as though she was miles away in the distance and not simply at the bottom of the stairs.

"Elliott, we can't let her go alone, come on," Mark grabbed Elliott by the arm and pulled him towards the bottom of the cellar stairs. The fog was starting to clear but he couldn't see Roisin, just the cold stone floor of the cellar through an eerie almost iridescent blue fog.

"Jump," Mark shouted, and as he did, his own voice sounded strange to his ears, as if it was the voice of someone else far away. Mark felt the cold stone against his knees as he landed on the cellar floor, it was dark and his eyes tried to adjust to the lack of light. He felt a hand on his arm, "Elliott?"

One week earlier

"You are staying with Nanny for the summer, I don't want to hear another word about it." That's what her mother had said, and when Roisin's mother said it was the last word, Roisin knew to protest any more would be pointless. They had been discussing it for a few weeks. When I say they, Roisin had heard her parents discussing it, it wasn't a decision she had made or indeed a decision she had any choice in.

Not that Roisin didn't want to spend the summer with her nanny, Roisin had a very close bond with her nanny and always felt that nanny knew her, not just in the familiar way, but Nanny knew when Roisin was upset, or afraid, even if no one else did, she could look at her nanny and she would just know exactly how she felt. This was like a blanket of security when she was young, but now Roisin was thirteen, and sometimes, she wasn't sure she wanted someone to know exactly what was going on in her mind.

Roisin and her younger brother Mark had spent many summers with Nanny and Grandad before, but this was when Nanny and Grandad lived in Ireland too. Nanny and Grandad had moved back to England three years ago to help look after their parents as they were getting older, they had moved back to Manchester into their old family home, a house that they had rented out for the last twenty-five years to strangers; the strangers had just left, no explanation.

Nanny had thought this was a sign…"It's time for us to go home," she had told Roisin, "but, we are only across the water, we will visit, and you can come to stay in the school holidays."

That was three years ago and she hadn't seen them since. She had regular telephone calls and FaceTime, when Nanny could work out which button to press, mostly they were FaceTime calls spent asking, "Where is the camera? I can't see your face?" so calls were better, no distraction by technology, or the lack of the ability to use it.

So it had been decided, Roisin and Mark would go to Nanny's for the summer. This was Roisin's last summer before secondary school; when she returned to Ireland, she would be going to the convent, a thought she did not relish. Although Roisin was a popular girl, she preferred the company of horses and dogs, spending all the spare time she was allowed with her paternal grandparents, Nanny and Grandpa O'Neill. They lived down the lane from Roisin's home and they had stables, and most importantly, horses.

It did not matter the weather, sun wind or rain (and in County Cavan in Ireland, there is a lot of rain) Roisin would be there, mucking out the horses at first light with Gypsy by her side. Gypsy was a black Labrador collie cross, she had been rescued from the local dog pound when Roisin was nine, and from that day to this, they were inseparable, Roisin thought Gypsy was more intelligent than most of the people she had met. She had never set out to train her, but somehow Gypsy just knew what to do and when. She was a beautiful gentle dog but fierce in her loyalty, no one could raise their voice or a hand in Roisin's presence if Gypsy was by her side, you would see her start to hunker down and the hairs on her back stand up, and she would make a low, unnerving growl as her lips started to peel back from her teeth. A pat on the head and a few gentle words from Roisin would calm her, but it was undeniable, she was Roisin's protector.

It was Roisin's last weekend in Ireland for a while, her mother would be driving Roisin and Mark to England on Monday morning. They were going to fly, but when Nanny had agreed to let Gypsy visit for the summer as well, the ferry was booked.

As Roisin walked up the lane to Nanny O'Neill's she wondered, what would there be in Manchester for her? A big city, tall buildings, no fields, no horses and lots of strangers. She shuddered at the thought; most thirteen-year-olds would be excited at the prospect: bright lights, modern city and the Trafford Centre, but not Roisin.

She opened the gate at the end of the lane, and waited for Gypsy to pass through before closing it behind her. She heard a familiar whinny from the top field, she looked up and there was Chip, flicking her head as if to say "I see you, here I am." Chip was a cheeky rather plump, looking chestnut pony at a less than statuesque fourteen hands. Roisin's mother insisted that Chip was plotting against them as she had that mischievous look in her eyes, her gaze always following and always watching.

As Roisin walked down the lane towards Nanny O'Neill's, the old box factory cast a large shadow and she felt the heat of the June sun disappear. It had once been a thriving hub of workers and deliveries and constant noise, but not any more. Mother nature had claimed the derelict site for herself and the once boldly painted, grey and black walls were now dull with peeling paint from decades of Cavan rain and sprawling ivy reaching to the very roof and beyond. Birds now nested in the rafters and you could see them emerging from the holes in the broken and rusted corrugated roof.

In the winter Roisin would be afraid to walk down the lane alone, even with Gypsy by her side, as the building loomed empty and foreboding and the sounds that came from within would send shivers down her spine.

"It's only the birds and bats," her brother Mark would say... He was not afraid of anything. Roisin had heard tales of the bats in the country getting tangled in your hair, old wives tale or not she would not walk past after dusk without her waist length hair very securely tied up!

As she approached Chip's field, she rubbed the worn leather of her bridle between her thumb and forefinger, liking the way the little pieces of dirty leather would rub away between them, allowing that familiar warm, leathery, pony smell to escape just a little. She would only need the bridal to hack the short walk back to the farm where she could groom her and get her tacked up. She could see Chip happily grazing with her head now stuck between the gaps in the gate; no matter how big the field she always wanted the grass that was just out of reach. The gate rattled as Chip freed herself from the gates, how the gate was still standing was a mystery given that the hinges had long since failed and now it was secured with old lead ropes. The familiar sound of the electric fence clicked as it earthed on long pieces of grass and overgrown bushes. This was part of the heartbeat of the farm that Roisin loved, the familiar sounds and smells, and she would miss these.

The usual battle of wits followed, with Chip refusing to put the bit in her mouth but always eventually giving in and opening her mouth. Roisin knew as well as Chip did that Chip wanted that bridal on as much as Roisin wanted her to put it on, but each time the same game ensued until Chip gave in. Chip wanted to go out on a hack as much as Roisin did, this was their time to be free. Methodically and almost without thinking Roisin finished the last of the buckles and then took the reins and Chip's mane in her left hand and vaulted effortlessly on to Chip's broad back. Together they wandered down the lane and towards the farm, no rush, relaxed reins held only at the buckle, both in tune with each other. People had always said Roisin had an affinity with animals, and they with her. She looked back to ensure Gypsy had taken up her usual position. There she was walking slowly behind in the middle of the lane, no one would be overtaking Chip without Gypsy giving a warning first… Not on Gypsy's watch.

They had been on the hack for about an hour and Roisin was tired so she knew Chip must be too. She could see the old oak tree ahead, they always rested here for a few minutes before returning to the farm. Roisin tied the reins loosely to some old bailing twine that had been on the fence for years and lay down on the grass. As her chest rose and fell, not out of breath but faster than resting pace, she breathed in deeply enjoying the smells that surrounded her: the damp grass, the smell of Chip so warm and earthy and as she closed her eyes she felt the hum of the earth beneath her. She had once tried to explain the *hum* to her mother, but without success. Her mother insisted it was her own heartbeat she could hear. Roisin thought otherwise, the sound was different and it wasn't just a sound it was feeling, deep inside like a vibration running through her veins or the feeling of a cat purring loudly, that is if the cat was inside the earth. It was not her heartbeat she just knew it.

Roisin opened her eyes with a start to a very loud, "SQUAWK!" It made her sit up with a bolt, she must have dozed off in the warm sun but she was sure she hadn't.

"SQUAWK!"

She turned around but found herself looking directly into the sun. As she used her hand to shield her eyes she saw him. "Hello, my old friend," she said to the rather magnificent looking crow that was standing on the grass beside them. His feathers were so glossy, the purest of black and so thick it almost looked as though he wore long trousers.

When Roisin's mother would throw scraps out to the birds, she would always shoo the crows. She called them scavengers, but Roisin thought they were beautiful and intelligent. She once lost her way on a Christmas hack through the forest at Killykeen in Cavan. She had seen a crow and followed it, sure enough, the crow had led her back to the bridal path. Roisin had a lot of respect for crows and she thought they felt the same for her. She reached into her bag and pulled out the remnants of a breakfast roll. She had heartily enjoyed the bacon and sausage, but had intentionally saved the crusty roll for her fine feathered friend. This couldn't be the same crow that had led her through the forest two years ago, but she liked to imagine it was and whenever they came to rest at the big oak tree since that day, the crow had appeared.

She broke up the roll into two large pieces. The crow hopped towards it and then bowed its head almost as a sign of gratitude, and then he quickly flew away with it in his beak. A few moments later he returned for the second piece, again he bowed his head in thanks, once more let out a SHRIEK and flew away. Roisin stretched, she was getting pins and needles in her feet now and needed to get moving. She gathered up her things and loosely took Chip's reins; they would walk together the last quarter mile back to the stables, it would give them time to talk. As she walked slowly down the lane, Gypsy following at the rear, the crow swooped effortlessly and gracefully overhead.

What a perfect afternoon this had been.

Chapter Two
Widdershins

Later that night Roisin packed the last of her belongings into her suitcase. She had a box of books that Nanny O'Neill had left at the house for her mother to take to England. Nanny was obsessed with books and she practically had her own library in the spare room in England. "It's not a spare room," Nanny had insisted, "It's my den."

Roisin looked through the box of books, Nanny would love these; Millers Guide to Antiques, 1001 Home Remedies, books on how to do just about anything, a strange looking book, much older than the rest and very dusty. Roisin picked it up and the cover felt like leather. She brushed away the dust from the cover, it made her sneeze. As she flicked through the pages it had that odour of old people, or newspapers that had been stored in the attic for many years and the pages were yellow and curling at the edges. She put the book back in the box as she had noticed something far more interesting, the book of Horse Knowledge. Nanny O'Neill must have put this one in for her.

Roisin picked up the book and turned on her heels, she would have a read of this one before her tea was ready. She grabbed the beanbag from the floor and threw it on the bed, arranged the other pillows around her and got herself nice and comfortable. As she sat back ready to lose herself between the pages of The book of Horse Knowledge, she realised the book in her hands was the old leather book, Widdershins.

Oh well she was comfortable now she may as well have a look, Roisin opened the book and began to read...

Widdershins Page 1

Read this book and read it well, Past secrets, it is waiting to tell, For you it was written one of three,

The one who's been resting beside the oak tree,

The curse that was placed 1300 years and no more, Is waiting to be lifted if you open the door.

Things that were there, remain to be found, Changed only in vision but not in sound.

If you listen, you will hear them - if you listen true. For they are talking - but only to you.

On the thirteenth solstice of their thirteenth summer, the sun will set,

Then the blood moon will eclipse the sun, and out of the darkness the light you will get, Three that were no more will be again and three that are new will go widdershins.

Do you know the difference with folklore and legend? These are the stories that are passed down through time, from person to person, generation to generation, but always within the legend is the truth. A tale so important it has been spoken about for hundreds of years, each story teller adding a little colour and an extra thread, but still the story remains true to its origin, that is true of Widdershins, once a place of great importance, not a place of greatness in size as it was a small, modest farm, hidden away in the oak forest, the oldest of the oak forests.

At a time when the country of England was yet unformed in an untamed area in Mercia, a new religion was taking over the land, the Pagans of the old religion found themselves hiding out in the forests, protecting the old ways, protecting the magic, protecting each other.

Nestling quietly in the oak forest beside Goderich brook was a small unassuming farmhouse, smoke wafted gently from the chimney, you could hear the chickens going about their business in the farmyard and the horses playfully chasing each other in the paddock.

The door to the farmhouse opened and their stood a strange looking lady, shawl around her shoulders and partly wrapped around her wispy white hair, she wore an apron tied around her waist with two large pockets on the front, as she put her hands on her hips a frog jumped out of her apron's pocket, "be gone now little fella" she said gently after him, "return when the moon is full and we will see if we can't fix your little problem" with that the frog hopped away and under the hedge. The strange looking lady walked down the pathway towards the forest, stopping now and again to pick a flower or a berry and place it in her apron. Her hair was white and wispy and yet her face was not aged or haggard, but soft and gentle, with soft grey eyes.

As she wandered towards a clearing in the woods, she could see the beams of sunlight bursting through the branches of the mighty oak, it was almost solstice, in 24 hours the sun would be perfectly aligned in the sky and the solstice stone would be bathed in the purest of light, recharging the woods for another cycle in the wheel of the year.

As she thought of this, her brow furrowed for she knew that they would be coming soon to try to take the stone. She could not allow this to happen, if the stone did not receive its charging light, the magic would fade, the darkness would creep in and the balance of nature and the world would be in danger.

There had been six stones originally and this was the last that remained.

Silas had the other five; each time he had found a stone he had reversed it preventing the sun from charging the stone and allowing it to absorb the dark light from the underworld.

She would meet with the forest folk before the solstice, as soon as her children were back from the hunt, but for now she sprinkled a circle of salt around the stones, muttered some words that sounded like a strange older language than even the writer of this legend had heard before.

As she turned to leave, a crow, beautiful, majestic and black with feathers so thick he appeared to be wearing trousers appeared in the clearing. "SQUAWK."

"Come on my friend, we have little time to prepare" the strange lady spoke to the crow as you would an old friend, and as the crow landed on her shoulder, together they walked back to the farm.

As she opened the door to the farm house the smell of the open fire was the first thing that you noticed, you could smell the wood burning and the smoky undertone as there was still green moss on the wood, the smoke was quite acrid at first to the point it would make your eyes sting, above the fire hung bunches of herbs and flowers, drying partly from the heat and partly from the smoke, a slick black cat lay near the hearth, glossy black coat but short haired with the smallest star of white under his chin, it almost made it appear as though it was his shirt peeping out of his slick black suit.

There were jars of liquids and powders lining shelves along the back wall and a rack with more flowers and herbs drying beside a doorway.

As your eyes adjusted to the dark, the room revealed itself like an Aladdin's cave of nooks and crannies and curiosity's.

As the strange lady knelt before the hearth she picked up a hand full of salt and threw it into the flames,

" Hear me now and hear me true, through the passage of time I'm talking to you"

She sat back on her heels and as she did the sound of chatter began to fill the room, from what was only a moment before an empty farmhouse kitchen, it now appeared more of a gathering, a gathering of what can only be described as the most unusual collection of characters straight out of a story book, these were indeed the strangest of forest folk.

The friends of the forest had heard the call and they knew that this night of all nights they would need to be at their best, for this was the night that darkness would come and if Silas had his way, darkness would stay.

The chatter in the room was one of a nervous hush. As if intentionally to dispel the nervousness in the air the crow flew into the room and as he opened his wings to land, there was a flurry of jet-black cloth and the wings were no more but instead there stood a young striking man, clothed in a rich black cape with hair as black as that of the crow's feathers, his face was pale and white with a very angular nose and his eyes were piercing yellow, bathed with thick black lashes. The door of the farmhouse opened fully with a gust of fresh forest air and in walked four extremely tall gentlemen, they appeared the same and yet somehow individual, the first one to enter the room, loomed tall above the forest folk and he had to lower his head and stoop slightly to allow for the beams of the kitchen ceiling as he entered , he carried a white staff in one hand, his hand curled over the top of the staff, long thin fingers and old yellow nails, his skin was pale and grey and wrinkled with age. His eyebrows that were just visible under the hood of his cape were long and white and wispy, as he removed his hood and looked at his host, you saw his gentle green eyes, so soft they made his face warm and friendly despite the cold wrinkled appearance of his skin.

"My Lady Isabella"

He said as he sat at one of the corner chairs of the kitchen table and smiled warmly at his host, a smile of friendship but also of worry.

"My Lord you are welcome"

Lady Isabella waved her hand to the three remaining corner chairs to direct the three other gentlemen to their seats, they would have to be seated as the four of them filled the small kitchen towering over the other guests. Lady Isabella turned to face her other guests, "Now the Guardians of the Quarters are here we may begin."

Chapter Three
Little brothers

Mark was eleven. He was a sturdy boy for eleven and already stood head and shoulders above Roisin, and he was quiet by nature and was one of those lucky people that never seemed to be in a bad mood, unless he was tired that is but he genuinely always saw the best in everyone. This worked to his advantage as he could get away with anything, all he had to do was look at you with those big wide eyes and beaming smile and you couldn't stay angry with him for more than a second. His demeanour was truly a blessing and if you knew him, you felt the warmth from it.

He lay on his bed looking at the trotting posters on his wall, that was his passion, and he was not only passionate about it but he was an excellent rider. His horse Missy was to him the most beautiful bay pony. His father had described her as 'a boring bay.' Mark could not understand how he could even think that of Missy with her beautiful glossy brown coat and black tail and mane. When he groomed her and braided her hair, to him she was a champion. She stood a mere 13.2 hands but she could move, her top speed had been recorded at 32 mph and her gait was paced, not square going.

He had never really shown interest in many subjects at school, preferring to be active rather than studying. He was a keen Gaelic football player and loved to work on the farm, and you wouldn't find him with his head in a book like his sister. He much preferred the movies, although he did enjoy it when Roisin read to him. She always had since they were small and this was their thing. Mark was very close to his sister and was such a young gentleman, he would always offer to carry her bags or help with the saddles, but when it came to the horses, there were no allowances made, the competition was on! They would often race through the fields at the back of Nanny O'Neill's, Chip versus Missy in the Grand National of the farm. If it was flat going, he had a chance but if they went steeplechase, Roisin would win. Missy was a road horse and disliked the jumps. He would miss that this summer and as he lay there still staring at his posters, he couldn't help but feel a little trepidation at what the summer would bring, but he was looking forward to seeing his nanny and grandad in England.

Hot chocolate! That was thought that broke the daydreaming for Mark, he hadn't been sleeping well for a few weeks now and one of his Mammy's hot chocolates might just help, with a sprinkle of cocoa on top and maybe one or three marshmallows; perfect. That would help he thought to himself and maybe he wouldn't have the strange dreams tonight. He wanted a good rest before the ferry tomorrow, and he felt the four tall strangers had disturbed his sleep for long enough.

The hot chocolate the night before hadn't worked and Mark was tired. He had slept a little in the car on the way to the ferry but it wasn't enough, he was grumpy. He tried to snap out of it as they pulled into the port and the sight of the ferries was enough to distract him temporarily. He had never been to a port before and he was very impressed with the huge shipping containers, the skyline was littered with cranes, bigger than anything he had seen before, and the ferries...

"Which one is ours, Mammy?" he asked as they pulled into line to await boarding. He hoped it wasn't the small one directly in front of them, not that there was anything wrong with the Jonathan Swift, it was a perfectly reasonable looking ferry but it was undeniable that it dwarfed in comparison to the mighty Ulysses that towered above and beyond it, he could see the lifeboats hanging from the side and the huge giant like winches on board. To Mark this was the equivalent to the Titanic. It was an ocean liner , not just a channel ferry, please let it be the Ulysses he thought as he stared up at the impressive vessel in front of him.

"We have to take the slow ferry as we need the kennels for Gypsy," his mother told him, but which is the slow one?

Mark could hardly contain his anticipation at the potential disappointment that would be revealed in the next sentence, "But which is the slow ferry?"

"The Ulysses" his mother answered. He sat back into his seat smiling smugly to himself. He couldn't wait to get on board and explore, as he closed his eyes and began to imagine being inside the engine room with the captain and the start of the engine of the car brought him back into the here and now.

They completed their boarding and secured Gypsy into the on-board kennels and made their way up the Sapphire stairs, "You kids run ahead and find us a good spot, somewhere with a table," their mother instructed.

Roisin and Mark looked at each other with that all knowing grin of devilment. They set off at the speed of light, up the stairs, they ran through the bar and past the duty free, then they came to the side area of a bar near a casino with a real Black Jack table and a few slot machines. There were tables with soft cushioned benches and best of all, they were beside the windows. The windows were round but misted with some form of long-term condensation, but they were good enough for the virgin sailors. They spread their coats and bags out as previously instructed by their mother and settled down to start their journey.

As the ferry pulled away from Dublin port and the land began to disappear into the distance, neither of them realised what was to come and how different they would both be the next time they stepped foot on the isle of Ireland.

Three and half hours that is how long the journey would take, they would arrive in England, or Wales as their mother had corrected them, at around twelve midday. It was only nine a.m. and it was time to explore. They fastened up their jackets under strict instructions that they couldn't go on deck without them and that they couldn't go on deck without each other. "If one of you goes overboard you need the other one to sound the alarm," their mother, as pragmatic as ever had insisted. "And don't spend all your money on plastic rubbish in the duty free, you have the whole summer to spend your money, make it last!"

As they walked between the aisles of seats, they could feel the sway of the ferry and the sea beneath them. It was a little unnerving at first as neither of them had got their sea legs, in fact the only venturing either of them had experienced was fishing for pike or bream on Town lake or Killykeen in a fourteen-foot boat, and this, well this was very different. Without saying a word, they were both heading to the upper deck, this was the exploration priority... get up on the deck.

As they forced open the heavy steel door to the viewing area the weight was the first thing that struck them, even with both of them pushing, it was a battle with the wind to fully open it, but just as they managed to push the heavy door open wide enough to fit through, the wind took control and whipped it open, both of them grabbing a hold of the handle as tight as they could to prevent it from slamming into the wall of the ferry. They gingerly stepped out onto the cold industrial steel deck, the lines and markings faded with wear and time and the ravages of the sea. It was a beautiful June morning and the sky was a deep-sea blue; was this really the reflection of the sea beneath them? Despite the good weather the wind was howling and gusting in their faces, thank goodness they had their jackets on. Mark looked at his sister and while the excitement of the possible danger and the extremity of the weather lit up his face and made his eyes wild with wonder, there was a different look on Roisin's face, it was one of pure terror!

"Don't look so pleased with yourself!" Roisin shouted to Mark and she had to shout to be heard over the wind that was whistling through her ears. "We could be blown away or washed overboard at any moment, I don't like it."

"Don't be afraid," Mark said comfortingly to his sister. He put his arm around her shoulder. Roisin wasn't sure if he had done this to comfort her, which it definitely did, or if he had done it to stop her blowing away and being washed out to sea. Mark squeezed Roisin's shoulder and steered her towards the edge,

"Mark, no, I really don't like it, I am afraid"

Mark could see that, but he was unsure if it was the wind that was making his sister's eyes water or if she was on the verge of tears. "Don't be afraid, nothing is going to happen to you, not on my watch." Mark turned to face his sister and gave her that beaming smile and squeezed her shoulders and she had to admit she did feel instantly safer. She turned her face to look up at Mark and tried to give a brave smile.

They walked together towards the railings, with Mark bolstering Roisin with his arm around her shoulder. Roisin hoped he wouldn't notice that she was walking with her eyes practically closed, squinting just enough so that she could see where her feet were landing but not enough to see over the edge, the kind of squinting she did when she tried to pretend she was brave enough to watch the scary movies with Mark but really she was watching his face to see when it was safe to open her eyes.

They stood at the railings and the spray from the sea carried with the wind and it stung as it hit their faces, the wind was breathtaking, Roisin opened one eye fully to peep and she could see the waves crashing around the ferry where it met the sea. It was a long way down, but she felt safe now with Mark stood beside her and even though it was still stomach churningly scary, it was worth seeing.

They looked at each other, eyes wide with adventure and both began to laugh. "Tell me little brother, what has you so grumpy today? Were you too excited to sleep?" Mark's brow furrowed at this question and as he looked at Roisin, she knew it was more than lack of sleep that was bothering him, "Mark," she squeezed his arm reassuringly, "you know you can talk to me, you can tell me anything."

Mark linked his sister's arm and guided her back to the huge steel doors. If he was going to tell her about the four strangers, he certainly wasn't about to start shouting on deck.

As they approached the steel doors, they could see someone in a long grey duffle coat with the hood pulled up, a frail looking possible elderly man. As the man started to open the ferry door he slipped, the heavy door was about to close and crush him between the frame and the door. Mark let go of Roisin's arm and leapt the few feet to quickly grab the door. The elderly person looked up and to Mark's surprise he wasn't elderly at all but there was something familiar about him, his hair was wispy and long, it was hard to tell if it was grey or blonde but his face was young and his eyes crystal clear and a deep blue that matched the ocean. The now not so elderly man looked at Mark and grabbed his arm. "Thank you, Mo Chara."

Mark stared at him. Why was he so familiar and why was he calling him Cara? Wasn't that a girl's name? Mark's eyes darted towards Roisin she was still where he left her a few feet from the door. The strange man squeezed Mark's arm and leaned in to whisper, "Do not be afraid of your dreams, my Chara."

Mark pulled the strange man's hand from his arm and turned to Roisin. "Did you hear that?" Mark said almost breathless with surprise.

"Hear what?" Roisin said looking quizzically at Mark.

"He said..."

As Mark turned to point to the strange man, he realised they were

24

alone again and the door was closed. He ran to the door and looked through the port hole window, but there was no one in sight.

"What is it Mark?" Roisin asked.

"It's nothing," he shrugged. "I think I'm over tired, I'm beginning to imagine things."

He laughed unconvincingly and gave her his best beaming smile, but Mark was unsettled by his brief encounter. He was sure he had met the stranger before, but where? There was that niggling doubt in the back of his mind that made him certain, he was not imagining anything. One thing he did know, he needed a nap.

Mark made a make-shift bed on the seats beside his mother, the leather was cold but the inside fleecy lining of his coat made a good pillow. As he lay there willing himself to sleep he could see the sky through the window of the ferry and a seagull flew by, how do they fly so far from land? he wondered to himself, but he didn't need to will sleep too hard as within moments his eyelids were so heavy they began to sting and as he blinked his eyes sleep came calling.

Mark quickly fell into a deep much needed sleep, you could see his chest rising and falling in a relaxed rhythm and his face became peaceful as he surrendered to his slumber.

As he drifted from the conscious to the surreal subconscious he found himself walking through a wood, though the trees were thick and dense, maybe this was a forest he thought to himself. The ground below him was damp and he could hear running water as though there was a stream or a brook nearby. He didn't recognise where he was or where he was going, but as is often the case in dreams he knew he had to keep going.

Mark heard a twig crack somewhere to his left. He stopped dead in his tracks and tried to look through the dense greenery but he could see nothing moving, he tilted his head just as a dog would to try and hear any sound on the wind but the was no sound; actually Mark noticed there was no sound at all, he couldn't hear any bird song and he could no longer hear the running water.

"Mo Chara," spoke a voice in hushed tones.

The voice was softly spoken and almost a whisper but the sound still startled Mark, the hairs on the back of his neck stood up and he swung around, fists flying.

"Mo Chara, a bheith ciuin! We have no time they will hear us, we have to go…NOW." The stranger spoke in Irish and Mark realised he understood every word as his mind translated the words effortlessly. "My friend, be quiet."

As Mark turned around, he was faced with a very tall, young man, with long wispy blonde hair. He wore a long grey cloak-like coat and he had the hood pulled up to the point that it almost covered his eyes, almost but they were eyes that couldn't be hidden, they were piercingly blue. Mark's mind was racing, who would hear them? Where were they going? Who was this man?

"I will explain everything, but for now you must come with me, we are not safe. Silas is coming please, Mo Chara, trust me"

Mark didn't know why but he knew that he could trust the stranger, they ran through the forest, stepping between the trees, ducking at the low branches and hurdling over fallen trees. Mark's heart was racing and he could hear his heart pounding in his ears. He could see a clearing up ahead, a clearing? Surely not, a clearing would make them easier to find but as they jumped between two very large and clearly very old oak trees, the sound around Mark's ears muffled and popped as though he were under water, for a second he felt sick.

As Mark regained his senses, he realised he was no longer in the forest but in what appeared to be a grey stoned tower. He looked around his eyes darting from one thing to another trying to take in as much as he could as quickly as he could. He could feel the adrenaline pumping through his veins and he noticed his shirt sticking to the back of his neck as he was sweating profusely from his race through the forest.

As his heart rate began to return to normal and his breathing was less laboured, he began to take in his surroundings with more clarity. He was in a room with no corners, the walls were made of a grey slate-like stone and the walls towered above his head. He could see a small slit window but it was far too high for him to see out of, he realised he actually could not see the ceiling. "How high was this tower?" Mark thought to himself. As he looked further into his surroundings, he could see two doorways, one appeared to be what he could only assume was the front door and the other, well, was it even a door if it was lying flat on the ground. "Would it still be a door or would it be a hatch?" he thought to himself. Curved shelves lined the walls and jars upon jars of what looked like water, there were stacked towers of books, covered in dust and Mark could see from the spines that some of them were in Irish, and what was that? He stepped closer and wiped the dust off the spine of one of the books, he was right? The book was entitled 'The Clan O'Neill' It must be a coincidence he thought, only then did he realise that he could hear water, he hadn't noticed it before as the sound of his own heartbeat had been so loud, but it was definitely there and not just a trickle, it sounded as though they were standing under a huge waterfall, thunderous and loud as though the walls were about to come crashing down around them with the force of nature. "Mo Chara," the tall young man spoke gently. This brought Mark immediately back to his senses and surroundings. He turned around and faced his companion, tentatively taking a step backwards just in case, but just in case, who was he kidding? There was nowhere to run even if he wanted to; unless that is he wanted to run around the room in circles!

"Mo Chara, we do not have long and I need to speak to you while my powers are so strong, please listen." The young man pointed to a stool with an animal fur draped over it, "Please sit"

Mark did as he was asked without question and positioned himself on the stool, the stool was higher than he thought and his feet didn't touch the floor.

"I can only speak to you when your mind is between the plains and your subconscious is in control of your mind, my powers are elemental and are strongest when I'm close to my element... water. Remember this if you need to contact me in the future. Do not be afraid of your dreams, this is the time that has been awaited through time and time again, we need your help Mark. I know you have many questions but for now, know my name is Siar, I am the Guardian of the Watchtower of the West and I am your friend as you were once mine, Mo Chara."

"Mark, Mark." Roisin shook her brother harder as he refused to wake.

"Mo Chara," said Mark as he opened his eyes. He looked around, surprised to find himself back on the ferry, was that a dream? It couldn't be, it was too real. He sat up with a jolt.

"Mark, you were speaking Irish?" Roisin replied questioningly.

She knew Mark hated Irish lessons at school.

Mark stared blankly back at his sister, "Why did you wake me?" Mark asked, he had wanted to stay there, wherever there was, even if it was a dream, he needed to know more about Siar.

"Because we are docking, I knew you wouldn't want to miss it."

As they made their way back up to the viewing deck, Mark tried to shake his encounter from his mind, it had to be a dream? But what about the man on deck who had called him Mo Chara? What about the forest and the tower?

Chapter Four
"And Elliott makes three..."

"Where is Elliott?" Kairen asked as she walked into her mother's kitchen. She could see her mother carefully pouring the piping hot jam into sterilised jars on the worktop, "Is that Apple jam?" she asked her mother. She was hoping it was, ever since her mother had come home to England she had made Jam from the giant apple tree in the back garden, she had made apple gin one year also, but it was so strong everyone was afraid to drink it.

"It is," her mother replied. "

I thought I had better stock up before the kids arrive, and Elliott has taken the metal detector over to Shin's farm. Old Isabella found a coin when he was over last week and it looks old, so he asked her could he take the detector."

Kairen shook her head. "That boy and history, why can't he concentrate on the present day instead of obsessing about the past, I blame you mother. Always talking about buried treasure and Kings and queens." Her mother turned around sharply and it was difficult to say if she was offended or pleased by those comments,

"It's not my fault he has a natural love of history, it's in his genes. I'm the same and my mother's the same, it's better than wasting his time with make believe computer games. He's a very clever boy and he has such an enquiring mind, he will do well. You watch, and besides he will be fine, he has taken Benjy with him and old Isabella is there. It's the summer holidays, let him enjoy them."

Elliott had set off for Shin's farm at around eight that morning; he had made a mini packed lunch the night before and also made a flask of hot chocolate. He hadn't mentioned this part to his mother, given that he could walk to Shin's farm within ten minutes door to door from Nanny's. She would only question why he needed lunch at all when he could just come back to the house. She didn't understand the quest, Nanny did.

Nanny had taken him on many metal detecting adventures since she had moved back to England four years ago, and they both knew, if you were on good ground, the last thing you wanted to do was leave it, mostly because if they were on an organised club dig, and other members knew you were on a great spot or had found something interesting, the minute you left they would be there, like vultures picking off the meat, finding your coins!

Old Isabella lived on the farm behind Nanny's house. She had a few horses and a lot of land. Her house was intriguing to Elliott, parts of it were said to date back to the 1500s and some of the books he had read on the local history said that it was the oldest building recorded in the area. It was marked on maps as far back as 1650 and it was still a farm then. Elliott thought if there was ever a chance that treasure would be found in his back yard, this was it, or at least in old Isabella's back yard.

Elliott often went to Shin's farm when he was at his nanny's and he had met old Isabella by chance one day while out walking with Benjy. On first meeting, he had been afraid, how foolish he felt now, but some of Nanny's neighbours had said that old Isabella was a witch. When Elliott saw her on that first day he knew why. As Elliott walked around one of the large oak trees on the farm, and it was larger than any tree he had encountered before, she was just there.

He had not seen or heard her approaching. Stood directly in front of him out of nowhere was a haggard looking old lady, dressed in jeans, wellington boots and an oversized cardigan, over the top of this was a white apron with two sack-like pockets on the front. He was so shocked at this initial sight, that he had frozen momentarily; it was only when Benjy started to bark and lick her hands he snapped out of his daze.

It was then he had realised that this lady was not so haggard at all, but actually in need of his help. Her hair was dishevelled and he could see twigs and a little bit of grass tangled up with the wisps of white hair and she appeared to have mud on her forehead. There were twigs and sticky bobs stuck to one of the sleeves of her cardigan and the palms of her hands were a sticky, dirty combination of mud and blood and on her head she wore a knitted hat, a type of Aztec Christmas pattern, the sort you see on Christmas jumpers with two plaited strings hanging down.

"Oh, I'm sorry for staring, where are my manners, are you OK?"

Elliott asked and then realised what a stupid question that was, of course, the lady was not all right she was injured and she was bleeding! His mind started to race, what should he do. Should he leave her and run for help?

"I have had better days if I am perfectly honest." Elliott was surprised by the lady's voice, it was soft and gentle and yet tired and quiet to the point, matter of fact like and yet it sounded much younger than she appeared.

"Can I help you? Do you want me to get the police? What has happened?"

"Calm down, young sir," the lady had replied. "There is no need to be calling anyone, but if you would be kind enough to walk with me back to the farmhouse I would greatly appreciate it. I have to admit I feel a little shaken, I have been a little clumsy I'm afraid and taken a tumble beside the brook. I had seen a lovely clump of comfrey and I wanted to take a few leaves to infuse later. Just as I reached out I lost my footing and slipped; luckily I was beside the western oak tree a-a-and he c-c-caught me," the lady stuttered slightly and then corrected herself. "I mean I caught the tree and was able to steady myself."

Elliott had walked the lady back to the farmhouse as any young gentleman would. They had walked across a huge paddock, it must have been at least fifty acres with a few shrubby looking hawthorn bushes growing randomly throughout and a small cluster of young oak trees in the middle. The lady told him that this was once a mighty oak forest, in the time before towns when the world was wise. He liked listening to her tales as they chatted along the way about the farm and local history and by the time they reached the farmhouse, the lady, who had by now introduced herself as Isabella was linking Elliott's arm walking and chatting like old friends.

From that day to this, which must be almost three years now, whenever Elliott was at Nanny's he would call over to old Isabella's and they would often chat beside the fireplace in the kitchen or walk the lands around the farm, exchanging stories. Elliott would often run errands for her or help with her harvest of vegetable crops and herbs she grew around the farmhouse. Elliott had never met anyone who knew so much about history, old Isabella was like an Oracle and Elliott was more than happy to listen to her for hours and hours absorbing her knowledge and immersing himself in tales of bygone times. It wasn't just stories he told his mother, she was a wise old woman. "That's why they call her a witch!" his mother had protested but Elliott thought she was wise of the lands and she had taught Elliott many things.

But this day old Isabella was not to be seen. It was a small fact he had neglected to mention to his mother or his nanny, just a detail. He had spoken to her a few days before and she had told him she was hoping her children were to visit in person soon and she had much to prepare, so he probably wouldn't see her for a day or two. He had thought it a strange thing to say at the time, 'in person." How else would they visit he had wondered, come to think of it he had never seen or met old Isabella's children in person or otherwise, that is apart from the horses, she always referred to them as her children, and the way she spoiled the three in the top paddock, they may as well have been her children. Before she had vanished to make her 'preparations' she had presented him with a hammered coin, the coin she had confirmed had been found beside the northern oak at the top of the farm and Elliott had asked if he could bring his nanny's metal detector to see if there was more. This was a thought that delighted him, it was his first solo metal detecting mission. He knew Nanny trusted him and she knew he would take care of the detector and after all, he was the one who had read the manual and watched the DVDs, and whenever he went out with Nanny, he was the one detecting while Nanny walked beside him. A point in fact, he considered himself quite the expert. He couldn't wait. "Come on, Benjy, we have treasure to find." Elliott called to his trusty companion. He thought something must be bothering Benjy, as he seemed distracted and he had been jittery all day, standing and barking at nothing and then chasing thin air.

As Elliott made his way towards the top paddock where the northern oak was situated his mind wandered to his own impending visitors. His cousins were arriving from Ireland today and whilst he knew all about them thanks to Nanny and the usual family Facebook connections, he had never met them in person, there were only a few weeks age difference between himself and Roisin and he hoped they would all get along. But to be frankly honest he had always considered them his country cousins, living on a farm, messing around with animals, he wondered how they would feel spending the summer in Manchester. His own mother had insisted that Ireland was just as modern as Manchester! Elliott very much doubted it, he had thought about going over to see them when his mother raised the subject as she often did after a glass of wine or a family FaceTime as he knew she missed her younger sister, Roisin and Mark's mother. But if it was that good, why hadn't she been back in all these years and why had Auntie Jess moved back to Manchester last year? And besides, Elliott would miss the city libraries, the book shops and the connectivity that you only get with a huge city, at least when he visited Nanny, he was only a bus ride out of Manchester. Manchester was great and he loved the city library and the science museum, but he was definitely a Yorkshire lad at heart and he always preferred to be home in Leeds.

Benjy started to growl as Elliott started to climb through the barbed wire fence into the top paddock. Elliott stood inside the top paddock looking out at Benjy who had remained on the other side. Benjy was now down on his hunkers and the skin stripped back to show his teeth. He was not what you would describe as a guard dog, he was a black and white bearded Collie that Nanny and Grandad had rescued from the pound when they lived in Ireland. He had been run over and left in the pound. You would never know to look at him that he had once been an unwanted, dirty and broken hobo; his hair was magnificent, like lion's mane that moved with him when he ran, but he bore the scar of his road accident as his tail was off centre. You couldn't really notice it when his hair was long, but if he had recently been clipped it was clear to see, he was quite an imposing dog Elliott thought as he looked at Benjy. He looked large and statuesque, but if you saw him when his hair was wet you would realise how deceptive his hair was as he was such a slight dog under all the hair.

Something had upset Benjy and for some reason he did not want to enter the top paddock, he remained crouched down and barking at thin air. The clouds gathered overhead and it felt like thunder was in the air, the humidity was high the last few weeks as this had been the hottest summer in forty years, but the air felt strange as though the clouds were gathering for something, Isabella would have known what this meant Elliott thought, she was so in tune with nature sometimes, he half believed she was a witch!

"Benjy! This is not the time to tune into your inner weather guru." Elliott spoke to Benjy as if a friend and not just an animal, but Elliott believed Benjy was a friend and not just an animal and he knew, it was a fact, that Benjy understood him.

"I will have to leave you here if you are going to be a diva, this is a solo mission for us, which, yes I know insinuates that it couldn't be a solo mission as there are two of us but solo mission for man and solo mission for my canine friend."

Elliott turned his back on Benjy and started to make his way towards the giant northern oak. There was a huge oak tree at the four compass points on Isabella's land, she had once told him they were the only remaining trees from the original oak forest, the whole area had once been covered in a dense forest. Elliott was glad they weren't all there today as he was out of breath walking the fields and hills as it was, if he had to carry all his equipment and also make his way through a thick forest, that may have been a little too much for eight a.m. on a Monday morning. As Elliott gingerly looked over his shoulder to see if his brave companion was following, he saw Benjy ducking below the bottom wire on the electric fence and chasing after him. As he approached the large oak tree X literally did mark the spot, as Isabella had promised there was a small X made from stones to the left of the tree. He parted himself from his luggage and the trusty detector and sat down for a well-earned snack.

As Elliott sipped his extremely hot but welcome chocolate drink and munched his way through his ham sandwich, it had to be ham as he would eat no other sandwich filling, he looked up at the clouds gathering above; they really were quite angry now or at least the ones directly above his head! Maybe being beside the tallest tree on a hill in a possible storm was not the best idea. The thought of an impending storm turned his mind to his cousins again, he hoped they would be off the boat before any storm hit them, if it hit them, he thought. Wales was a couple of hours away on the motorway, he had been many times with Nanny and his mum metal detecting. He wondered if either of his cousins shared his love of history or treasure hunting, and if they would become friends. A roll of thunder overhead brought Elliott back to the present; he looked skyward again and was more than concerned at the thunderous clouds gathering above his head. He jumped into action and set up the detector, he would detect for an hour and hope the storm would pass, if not he would have to come back tomorrow... maybe with his cousins.

As he swung the detector from left to right, he imagined Roman coins and hordes of gold that could be hidden beneath the ground. "Ding." He stopped in his tracks as the detector rang out, he ran the detector over the same ground again, he knew by now to ignore anything less than a double ding, a double ding always meant there was something good hidden in the ground, even if it was a modern coin, it was still treasure. "Ding, ding, ding." Elliott couldn't believe it. "Benjy, did you hear that? we got a triple ding!"

He took his detector probe from his backpack and ran it over the ground where the detector had identified, immediately it started to vibrate, as he dug down a little with his trowel he heard a metal scrape; tentatively he began to remove the earth a trowel full at a time and place it on the ground beside him, checking it each time with the probe, no, it was still in the hole. He dug a little deeper and took a little more earth and placed it beside him. The probe went crazy, almost vibrating out of his hand. As he gently moved the pile of earth something glistened in the light. He picked it up and it looked like a dirty old stone. He then realised there was a thick chain attached to it, he rubbed it against his jumper to clean it and he could see it was a pendant, a watery looking yellow and orange stone set in some kind of metal mount. As he rubbed the stone with his thumb, lightning struck the giant northern oak, Elliott was thrown to the ground as a terrifying crackling sound and the smell of burning wood filled the air. He could hear Benjy barking frantically and just made out a tall shadowy figure standing over him before he passed out.

Chapter Five
Old Isabella

Old Isabella stood at the small window in the kitchen, from there she could see up into the top paddock. She could see Elliott on the other side of the barbed wire fence, it looked as though he was talking to his dog. That dog was a strange one old Isabella thought, but a good one, so loyal to that boy, he had been there the day she met Elliott.

From that very first day she had thought he may be a Darach, and after all, he would be thirteen this year with his thirteenth solstice this very year when a solar eclipse and a lunar blood moon eclipsed in the same month. It couldn't be a coincidence, but she had withheld her excitement as he was only one, for the veil to be lifted there would need to be three. When Elliott had told her about his cousins, the O'Neills, then she knew, she laughed out loud to herself and held her ribs as she remembered the day he told her, she knew then, it was time, it was finally time. The O'Neills no less; oh, old Isabella knew them from old, a mighty Clan who were greatly respected. Elliott was a clever young man, but he would need more than brains to fulfil the prophecy he would need to let go of his logical mind and align with the elements. She had given him the clue, the coin, she knew he would hunt for more, and if he was the one he would find the amulet, it could only be found by them, the chosen ones, the Darach Nua. But he would need help, he would need their help.

She looked up again and saw Elliott and Benjy almost at the Northern Oak. She walked over to the fire-place where a cast iron cooking pot was simmering away. She stirred the pot and threw in a handful of herbs, the pot bubbled almost to the point that it over-flowed but the contents remained within. She reached above the fire and took down a jar marked 'thyme 1600' took out a pinch and added it to the pot as she did she continued to stir and recited the words:

A pinch of thyme to step through time,
To thin the veil and return what was mine, Three that are no more

will be again, Three that are new will go widdershins.

She placed the jar back on the shelf and removed another jar, this one was labelled 'thyme 1700'. As she repeated the process the pot boiled furiously. She looked down as there was a familiar rub against her ankles. There was Oslo weaving in and out of her ankles, he was such a beautiful cat, so slick and black with his little white tuft; she often thought it looked as though he were wearing a tuxedo.

"This is not for you, my beautiful boy, I may have some scraps for you later, do what you do best and keep the rats from the kitchen and I may treat you. The time is coming and the rats are watching, keep them out of sight, my boy."

Isabella had waited a long time to make this brew. Thyme collected over the centuries to create a passage back, on long nights when she was all alone, she had often wondered, would the time ever come when she would need to make it, would the pieces fall into place? Would the veil ever be lifted? It had been so long at times it felt like a memory. But the time was now; they were coming home, but so many preparations first.

She wanted to watch through the window to ensure Elliott found the amulet, to help in any way she could, but she knew it was out of her hands now. If she interfered in any way, she could break the flow. The clouds had been gathering all morning, there was electricity in the air, this was a culmination of the elements uniting against the darkness and when the three finally came together in one place and one time there would be an almighty clash. This storm was coming, it had been simmering between the times for generations and now it had started nothing could stop it. Good versus evil, light versus dark, the battle that had existed before time had begun and there was a battle coming, and this one, they had to win.

Silas was returning she could feel his strength growing, it was like a cold damp fog that seeped into your bones but she could also feel the guardians awakening and that, oh that, was like a warm summer sun touching your bare skin after a cold winter.

She thought of Elliott and his cousins. They didn't know it yet, to them it was just another Monday on a beautiful June morning. They didn't know how long she had waited for them to arrive, and arrive they would, but would they be ready in time? It was only a few days to the solstice. She chuckled to herself. Children and in fact, adults today had no idea of the truth, to them the old ways were all myth and legend, tales to be told beside the campfire. She knew this was partly her fault, after all, she was the one who created the veil. Yes, yes, they would be fine, they just needed to work fast and while she was forbidden from offering information, she was also sworn never to lie to a Darach, even Darach Nua, so if a question was asked, she would answer it truthfully. The three of them may be young but their bloodline was rich and royal in the old religion, growing with strength through each generation for thirteen hundred years until the three that had the gift were aligned with the sun and the moon and the gifts, they were born to inherit but that slept sleepily within them, biding their time until the time was right were reignited allowing their power to rise. The rising of the Darach Nua.

Her mind was wandering and as a huge crack of lightning sounded from the top paddock and lit up the dark kitchen, she knew it had begun. He had found it and they had found him. Good work, Elliott, she thought to herself and smiled as she reached up for a jar with the label 'thyme 1800' only two more centuries of thyme to go and the potion would be complete.

She had been planning this day in her mind for so long, she could hardly believe it was here. Things were happening now that could not be stopped, not that she wanted them to, but when she cast the spell all those years ago, she was unsure of its strength, whether it would stand the test of time and whether it was strong enough to subdue Silas. Clearly it had been, now she had to make sure everything went to plan to heal the past and protect the future.

She would need to call a meeting, it had been thirteen hundred years since the last meeting and so many of the forest folk were sleeping, but at least when the veil was lifted, they would awaken. Isabella frowned again. There was no way around it, when the veil lifted, unfortunately it would not only be good that would be awakened but also evil. They had to be sure their plan was perfect so they were ready for the awakening and could contain the evil. It was the only way to bring the stone into the light and stop the darkness that was eating away at the world, and hopefully, one by one, that could regain the solstice stones.

Isabella finished her potion and removed the pot from the heat. She decanted the liquid into three small green vials. She then decanted more liquid into three small red bottles, and each green vial was sealed with a small brown cork and dipped into wax to create a perfect seal. She wrote on each label of the green bottles 718. Isabella then took some thyme from her pocket she had collected that morning. She added a little to each of the red vials and sealed them in the same way, on each of these labels, she wrote 2018. The remainder of the potionwas poured into a large stone jar, corked and sealed with wax.

She put the six vials in her apron, three green in one pocket, three red in the other and then she picked up the large stone jar and placed it on her hip as though she were carrying a small child. She carried the jar into a room at the back of the kitchen, the door was covered with a heavy red velvet curtain. Isabella balanced the jar on one hip as she drew back the curtain and opened the heavy wooden door. There were no windows in the room and as Isabella placed the stone jar on a table just inside the room, she spoke clearly. "Suth light the way, Suth banish the darkness from this day."

She clicked her fingers against the candle on the table and it illuminated instantly. The light that came from the thick red pillar candle filled the room, brighter than that of any electrical bulb; one candle and the room was lit as if by a beacon. Isabella closed the door behind her and sighed, half with relief and half with comfort, this room was her sanctuary. In this room, time had stood still; in this room the magic remained, untouched by centuries of so-called progression. In the centre of the room was a large book stand on which rested a large, heavy leather bound book, in beautiful golden calligraphy on the cover were the words 'The book of Time.'

Isabella walked over to the book, she stroked the cover of the book with familiarity, she then started to turn the pages, and it took two hands to turn more than one at a time, as the pages were so big. She lay the book open on a page with very little writing on it. At the top of the page it was written 'Darach Nua'. Isabella picked up the pen to add the day's events but stopped; she looked deep in thought and then started to turn the pages back again. This time when she stopped, the pages that were open were filled with words top to bottom. At the top of the page was the word 'Widdershins'. Isabella lifted the book down and placed it on the table beside a very comfortable looking rocking chair. She picked up a shawl that was over the back of her chair and sat down to read. If the same mistakes were not to be made again she had better remind herself of the last days and read this chapter again, it had been a while since she had revisited the past, so long ago in fact that the memory was hazy. It almost felt like it hadn't happened at all and it may have been a myth or legend. But then aren't all myths and legends a hazy memory passed through time?

Widdershins

Silas had been such a bright young man with such a promising future. He was eager to learn and helpful to all around him and his interest in the powers that he was to inherit was immense. More so than his siblings, of course they were all excited for their thirteenth summer and their thirteenth solstice. As children they were told tales of the Darach Nua, the 'New Oaks' as they were known. It was a gift to behold and one that was held in great esteem amongst the gifted community, the ability to communicate with nature, the animals, the trees, the forest folk but to always be guided by the wise Guardians of the Quarters and the Keeper of Time, to work with them to keep the balance.

For Silas it was more than excited anticipation, it was his life focus even before it was his turn to inherit his powers. He worked tirelessly to study the old laws, to read every enchantment and every spell that he could, he couldn't use them yet but he knew that day was coming. He studied plants and herbs and the power of the elements. When the time came for his siblings to inherit their powers he was only eleven years old. Silas still had two more years to wait. There would be a celebration in the forest, despite the fact that times were changing and it was not possible to celebrate freely as they had in the past, the forest folk and their Guardians, the Quarters and the Darach now had to live in the shadows of the forest and hide their powers from the Dall.

The Dall were the non-believers as now as they were the blind folk and could not see the truth, and they had been turned against them. It wasn't their fault, a new church and a new royal power had been sweeping Mercia for two hundred years, convincing them the old way was dark and not to be trusted, telling tales of bad magic and punishing those who were found to be sympathetic to the Darach. They convinced the Dall that any kind of magic was not natural; through fear and punishment over centuries they had somehow convinced the Dall that nature's magic was unnatural? These were dark times.

Silas' siblings were preparing for their double celebration, this only happened every thirteen hundred years and no amount of persecution from the Dall would stop this; his siblings were twins maybe this was why he had always felt slightly on the outside. They never left him out but they were different to him and just weren't as dedicated to their craft in the same way that he was. They were happy to wait to see which powers would be bestowed upon them. This was not enough for Silas he wanted to enhance his powers; he wanted to build all his knowledge in anticipation of his gift to ensure that whatever was bestowed upon him he could use to its maximum ability.

He couldn't help but wonder which gift he would receive, would there be only one? He hoped not for he had shown dedication for many years to learn the old ways and thought he deserved more.

The preparations were underway for the celebration. There was a real buzz of excitement in the forest as the solstice was almost upon them. It was Litha, midsummer, when the sun reaches its highest point in the sky and it's also the day with the longest hours of daylight, and when darkness comes the skies would be lit by the celebration fires and an offering made to the Sun.

Silas was helping to build the blessing passage, and it really was a passage, a rite of passage, those who were lucky enough to have the opportunity to walk through this were never the same when they came out the other side and their names would be recorded in the Book of Time from then until eternity. The passage itself was a walkway dug into the earth, creating a channel to allow the air to pass through. It was lined on either side with fires and ended in front of Goderich Brook. During the celebrations just before sunrise, fires would be lit to line the passage and as the Darach Nua walked through the passage in the earth with the air travelling with them and the fires burning on either side they were touched by the elements themselves. To complete the ritual they would be baptised in Goderich brook, you would know the true Darach Nua, the true of heart as the baptism required them to be held under water for thirteen seconds, and when they arose from the brook, their eyes would have been transformed to the greenest of green, a reflection nature and all her glory and the deeper the green the stronger the powers the

41

elements had gifted them. They would then surround the solstice stone and await for sunrise on a new dawn of a new day as the true Darach Nua. It was said that everyone walking the earth with green eyes was in some way related to the Darach.

Silas could feel the enormity of the event building in the air it was like electricity, as he carefully swept and sculpted the earth to create the steps down into the passage. He could hardly contain his anticipation.

Finally, the solstice was upon them, the celebrations went on into the night, feasting and fires and the exchanging of stories and legends until finally it was time for the blessing.

Silas watched and waited as his siblings made the walk through the passage, he thought his sister's hair would catch alight as it blew all around her as they passed through the flames. His brother and sister looked animated in the light of the flames, as they stood at the end of the passage, they took each other's hands and walked into Goderich brook.

The following day Silas thought the whole thing felt like an anti-climax, other than his siblings having beautiful deep green eyes he could see no difference; they did not appear magical or blessed to him. He thought it such a waste, in fact he did not think they deserved the title Darach Nua at all. He vowed to himself that his blessing would be different.

The following days passed by without incident, his siblings were learning how to use their gifted powers. His sister had been gifted with sight, she hadn't mastered it fully as yet but with help from the Keeper of Time she could look into the past and see mankinds memories. In time, with work, she should be able to see the future as well. His brother had been gifted unity with all animals; again it would take time to fully control his new powers but he had mastered entering the mind of a crow and again in time, he would be able to unite with all animals and see through their eyes. Their lack of ability frustrated Silas and he often thought but never said, the Darach Nua would be stronger if all the gifts were given to him.

Isabella took a bunch of thyme from her pocket to mark the page. As she closed the book she wiped a tear from her eyes. It was painful to remember the past, to remember how things were. She would finish this chapter later. She sat at the table and put her head in her hands and gently sobbed.

Chapter Six
Three that are new

The clouds were gathering overhead as they drove off the ferry into Holyhead Port, at least they were on dry land now Roisin thought. She had been worried that they would be caught up in a storm out at sea, but as she looked out over the sea the clouds had calmed and the blue sky looked beautiful and clear, more than could be said for the clouds currently overhead, black and thunderous and angry looking.

"It appears we are taking the Irish weather with us to Nanny's," Roisin said aloud but she received no response from anyone.

Mark had his face pressed against the glass of the window staring out to sea and her mother was manoeuvring the lanes through the port.

Gypsy looked up at Roisin and licked her hand, "At least you are listening to me" Roisin rubbed Gypsy's head and as she did Gypsy lay back down in the foot-well, panting as though she were about to take her last breath. "Can I open the window, Gypsy seems really warm?" Roisin asked.

"Not until we are out of the port, she will only try and stick her head out of it and get us all arrested," her mother replied.

Roisin slumped back into her seat. As she did her backpack poked into her spine. She struggled to take it off whilst still wearing her seatbelt and carefully released the lock, as soon as she did the car started to beep.

"Who has taken their seat belt off?" her mother snapped from the front. Roisin quickly manoeuvred her arms out of the back pack and replaced the seat belt. "Sorry, I couldn't get my bag off, it's back on now".

Finally free of the spine-poking bag, Roisin opened the bag and removed the old leather book she had been reading the night before. As she opened the book hoping to pick up the story where she left off, she turned page after page but each time it revealed nothing but a blank, yellowed page. No words adorned the pages as they had the night before.

She frantically turned all the pages; she had read it, only the night before? This was ridiculous! Where were the words? She closed the book and looked at the cover. 'Widdershins' it appeared to be the same book? She turned over the book to look at the back, she hadn't noticed the verse on the back before, but then she hadn't looked for it either.

"To read this book and read it right, you must only read it when the moon is bright." Siar.

Roisin stared at the verse, this made no sense? What did it mean? How could there be a book you could only read at night? "Mark," Roisin whispered. Mark continued to stare out of the window and into the sea.

"Mark." This time her voice was much sterner and accompanied by a dig in the ribs.

"Hey, there is no need for that," complained Mark and genuinely looked offended at his sister's aggression. "Why are you whispering?" he asked while rubbing the site of his injury.

"Have you switched my book?" Roisin asked accusingly, she knew he must have. It was the only thing that made sense. Pages do not disappear and you can read a book any time you like!

"What book? You know I don't read books, I haven't touched it?" Mark protested

"This book," Roisin replied pushing the old leather book towards Mark,

"Then how can I have taken it if it's here in your hands?" Mark took the book from Roisin. "Widdershins? What a storybook? Why would I want it?"

Mark turned the large leather book over in his hands, he had to admit he liked the way the leather felt, but he would never admit that to his sister.

"What? Where did you get this?" Mark asked Roisin, completely losing his train of thought and line of defence. His voice had changed from denial to accusatory; he looked at the inscription on the back cover, he couldn't believe his eyes. He ran his fingers over the letters to make sure they were real, as he traced the letters with his fingers he felt a strange cold sweat creeping up the inside of his collar. He read the words again whilst tracing them with his finger:

"To read this book and read it right, you must only read it when the

moon is bright," Siar.

"Roisin, tell me where you got this book." He paused and looked at Roisin, searching her face for a clue. "Have you met Siar too?" he asked tentatively.

Roisin stared back at him blankly, confused,

"Who is Siar?" she asked taking the book back and reading the inscription again for herself. "Mark? Tell me what or who you are talking about."

The car was almost at a standstill in the traffic now and their mother snapped both their attentions back into the moment. "Look. Look at the side of the bridge, there are lions on this side as you enter England but if you look behind as we travel under the bridge you will see dragons as you enter Wales."

Roisin and Mark both looked at the Lions, beautifully set into the side of the bridge, but just at this moment they were not thinking about the lions or dragons.

Thunder rolled overhead and for a second the sky lit up under a blanket of lightning, then more thunder bellowed out. Gypsy jumped up onto the seat between Mark and Roisin and began to whimper. Both Mark and Roisin instinctively reached out to put their hands on Gypsy to comfort her. The heavens opened as though there was a tear in the sky and all of the rain fell out directly on top of their car. Their mother turned up the windscreen wipers to double speed. "Don't panic, kids, it's just a storm shower it will pass, we will be at Nanny's in an hour."

Mark looked at Roisin. "What did you mean, have I switched your book? You have your book in your hand I don't understand?"

Roisin stared back at Mark whilst still comforting Gypsy and holding onto her book with the other hand. "Yes, I have this book, but when I read it last night it was this book but with a story in it and now I just have this book that looks like my book that has nothing but pictures in it? I thought you may have switched it."

"Switched it for what?" Mark protested. "Another really old, odd looking leather book that I just happened to have in my backpack with my sandwiches? Get a grip, Roisin."

The colour was rising in Roisin's face, it was unlike Mark to be so dismissive of her and she knew he was not telling her the whole truth.

"Don't tell me to get a grip," Roisin replied angrily. "You know something, who is Siar? And, what do you mean have I met him too? Who is he? Do you have a book too?"

Mark thought for a moment before he answered, whichever way he explained it, he sounded a bit crazy, but then, did he sound any crazier than Roisin with her disappearing book swapping story.

Mark took a deep breath and turned to look at Roisin. "I was going to tell you on the boat, when we were on deck, you asked me what was wrong."

"I remember," Roisin said. "Then you stopped to help that old man."

"Don't interrupt me."

Mark replied. "If I'm going to tell you, you are going to listen, I will start at the beginning, please don't interrupt until I have finished, but then you need to tell me about the book,"

"Deal," Roisin replied and they did the pinkie promise.

Mark told Roisin about the weeks leading up to today: his broken sleep, the four tall strangers that he never saw but were always there, lurking in his dreams. He told her he had been afraid to sleep but he didn't know why, he was never afraid in his dreams and they never felt like he was having a nightmare but whenever he awoke, their silhouette was imprinted on his mind.

"Mark, you should have told me."

"No interrupting," Mark replied to his sister. "I haven't finished yet."

Roisin put her hand over her mouth as if to emphasise that she wouldn't speak again until he had finished.

Mark continued on and told her about the young stranger whom he met on the boat and who, he had initially thought was old. He looked at his sister trying to judge her reaction, but she was listening intently, not judgingly, so he continued.

Mark told her about his dream, where he was in the forest running from Silas with his new companion, Siar. He described the tower where Siar had taken him and how Siar spoke to him in Irish and he understood every word. The sound of water everywhere as though they were inside a waterfall and that Siar had told him he needed Mark's help as he had helped Mark before.

"Don't stop, what happened next?"

Roisin's eyes were wide open and not with disbelief but with anticipation of what he was about to say next.

"That's it," mark replied,

"What do you mean that' it?" Roisin replied shortly "That can't be it?"

Mark shook his head. "That is it, you woke me up."

There was silence in the back of the car, they both just stared at Gypsy thinking, stroking her head soothingly, absorbing what Mark had said. Thunder rolled overhead again and this time an almighty crack filled their ears as fork lightning struck the fields in the distance. The storm seemed to be travelling with them.

"Half an hour, kids, and we will be out of this storm and at Nanny's," Roisin and Mark barely noticed the storm.

"Your turn," Mark said to Roisin. "Tell me the story that disappeared." Roisin clasped her hands together and gave Mark the serious face, the one she gave him when she was explaining why his opinion was wrong or irrelevant.

"Well it started with a weird rhyme."

"What rhyme? What did it say?" Mark asked eagerly.

"No interrupting remember, and besides I didn't memorise it, it was something about thirteen hundred years ago and things that were new and things that were old, oh and there was something about the sun and the moon, I remember it had solstice in."

"What's a solstice and…" Mark quickly covered his mouth as he remembered the rules he had created. "Sorry no more questions until you are finished."

Roisin went on in great detail for someone who hadn't memorised the book. She told him there had been an oak forest somewhere in old England near Manchester, and in that forest lived an old lady by the name of Isabella. Isabella was sort of a magic woman or witch. Roisin wasn't sure as she hadn't read enough, but the lady was protecting a stone from someone called Silas,

"Oh my God!" Mark couldn't help himself from interrupting, the coincidence was too much. "You said Silas, that's who I was running from in my dream with Siar."

"Mark, do you want me to finish the story or not? Now I forget where

I am up to." Mark dutifully put his hand over his mouth and waited.

"The old lady, Isabella, was having a meeting with forest people, oh and she could talk to frogs and I'm not sure why but she was throwing salt everywhere, and then they all had a meeting in her kitchen, and at the end the last four people came in so the meeting could start. Four really tall men who had to bend down because either the roof was too low or they really were really tall, oh and I forgot the crow who was actually a man and I think the tall men were guardians of something."

Roisin took a deep breath; she had got quite carried away reciting the story to Mark and had even surprised herself how much she had remembered.

"Is that it, are you finished?" Mark asked and paused patiently.

"Yes, except there were a few stones I think, before, but not any more the old lady only had one left."

They both sat back in silence, thinking about the information the other had given them. Mark looked out of the window and realised they were no longer on the motorway. "How long till we're there?" he asked.

"You two have been so busy chattering to each other that we are almost here; we are in Pennington so about ten minutes. Get your shoes on and put everything in your backpacks"

Roisin looked at Mark, she took hold of his hand and squeezed, "Little brother, something very strange is going on, but I think, and I hope you agree, we tell no one until we have worked out exactly what this is?"

"Agreed," Mark replied adamantly. "And besides," he added, "They would definitely think we have lost the plot."

They shook on a pinkie promise.

"Put our book safe," Mark said to Roisin. "Oh it's our book now?" she replied,

"Well it would seem like it has something to do with the both us," Mark snapped.

"Calm down, little brother, I was only joking, it's going in the backpack until we can check it out tonight; do you think night time is enough or do we need a full moon?"

"I don't know," Mark replied looking deep in thought. "We may have another problem." He looked at Roisin as he said this, then they both spoke at the same time as they realised they would not be alone tonight.

Elliott felt the damp of his clothes before he fully realised where he was. It was like waking up from a sleep over and you didn't quite know where you were, but you knew it wasn't your own bed. He could feel the cold denim against his legs and realised he was shivering. His mind started to race, wet clothes, branches overhead, thunder in the distance.

Like a scene from a movie, his mind raced over the facts to catch up with reality. He sat up with a bolt, hand still tightly wrapped around his treasure, he could smell smouldering wood.

His mind started to clear and he remembered the tall shadowy figure he had seen before he blacked out. He jumped to his feet, assumed the fighting position and looked around him. He didn't know a lot of martial arts but Nanny had taught him the rudiments of self-defence.

Nanny had been an instructor once but now Elliott was her only pupil and he was ready, knife hand to the throat, that would stop any would be attacker.

"If they can't breathe they can't chase you," Nanny had told him sternly. "And if it comes to a choice between you and them, I choose you."

He was ready, open hands ready to strike, but there was no one around, no one that is except Benjy. Benjy was watching Elliott with great amusement, his head tilted on one side as though he was trying to work out exactly what was going on. Benjy seemed to decide that this was a game and Elliott's flailing arms were an invitation to play. He bounded over to Elliott jumping at his hands each time he moved them barking furiously with excitement.

"Stop, Benjy! They could still be here."

Elliott's eyes darted around while Benjy continued to jump around like a puppy enjoying the new game. Elliott looked at Benjy bounding around and realised how ridiculous he himself currently looked, posed to imitate the great Bruce Lee. He started to laugh, he saw the broken branch, burnt at the point the lightning had struck it from the tree on the ground beside him, and he laughed more. He sat back on the wet grass, this time unconcerned by the damp and gave Benjy a vigorous rub on the head.

He looked around at the empty field, he was all alone. It was then he realised he must have been gone for hours. He quickly checked his hand to make sure he hadn't lost his treasure, it was still there, the chain wrapped around the palm of his hand and the pendant glinting in the sun. Just wait till he showed Nanny his greatest find ever but, no, he thought he should show Isabella first and she wasn't around today; maybe he would keep it a secret just until he had the chance to show Isabella, and that way Nanny would let him come back tomorrow.

Tomorrow that was another day and he may not be alone, his cousins! He looked at his watch, twelve thirty. He needed to get back to Nanny's now, he was supposed to be there to meet them.

Elliott carefully filled in his excavation site, not that it was much of an excavation but those were the rules, you never leave a hole in anyone's land if they are good enough to let you dig. He trod the earth down over the now filled in hole and re-marked it with the cross of stones Isabella had left. He packed his bag ready to head off down the paddock.

"Benjy! Come on it's time you met Gypsy."

As Elliott zipped his trowel into his bag he leaned on the trunk of the giant oak tree, his hand found no resistance and carried on through the bark. Before he knew what was happening, he was laying face down in the earth, it was dark and smelled like Nanny's compost heap. Quickly scrambling to his feet he could hear Benjy barking behind the wall, well, if it was a wall he wasn't quite sure what it was. He felt it with his hands and it felt like the tree? He frantically felt up and down the tree wall, there must be a gap, how else could he have fallen into the tree?

"Elliott."

He stopped still and motionless, he had heard it as clear as day but now he wanted to un-hear it.

"Elliott."

There it was again, the voice from the darkness was deep and earthy and yet somehow familiar.

"Elliott, my name is Tuath, I will not harm you."

Elliott remained statuesque, afraid to move, in fact closer to the truth he was afraid to look. Had he banged his head when he fell he thought? He must be hallucinating. Is that even possible? He asked himself, could you hallucinate with your ears?

"Elliott."

He felt the tree wall with his hands and backed up tight against it. He squinted his eyes to try and see in the pitch black, but it was then he realised it wasn't completely pitch black he could see a glimmer of a light, down the corridor. Corridor, he scolded himself mentally, what was he thinking there is no corridor, he had just fallen through the gap in an old tree. But his eyes did not deceive him; he could see the flicker of a candle in the distance.

Elliott had watched many Criminal Minds episodes and he thought if ever there was a time he could possibly benefit from a psychotic break, this was it, he didn't like it and his logical mind was reeling.

He couldn't be in a tree and worse than that the tree could not talk to him.

"Elliott."

There it was again. Elliott covered his ears he wasn't listening any more, this wasn't happening, he began to hum to himself so he could not hear the tree any more.

"ELLIOTT I AM NOT A TREE."

Now Elliott was really concerned, the tree could read his mind.

"Elliott, open your eyes."

Elliott slowly moved his hands from ears to his eyes and peeped tentatively through his fingers. Stood directly in front of him was an extremely tall gentleman wearing a long green coat with long triangular shaped sleeves. It was embroidered with leaves in a beautiful golden thread. Beneath the coat there was what Elliott could only describe as a dress, it was floor length and black and peeping out of the bottom were the dirtiest, grimiest looking sandals and toes Elliott had ever seen, not that he considered himself a toe expert or sandal expert for that matter but these were definitely bad. He slowly lifted his gaze from the grubby feet and tried to peep through his eyebrows without actually raising his head.

"Elliott, my name is Tuath, I will not harm you, I am here because you have called me."

"I did no such thing!" Elliott blurted out defensively.

The tall gentleman let out a sigh and folded his thin bony arms across his chest, the veins sticking out as though they were on the outside of his skin and a smattering of white hair across the backs of his hands.

"Elliott."

The voice continued and now the tone sounded as though he may be losing patience with Elliott, his voice was soft and gentle and yet also tired and laced with exhaustion.

"You found the amulet, when you did, the door was opened."

Elliott wished he did not know what the man was taking about as this all seemed far too impossible to be real, but even as he ran these thoughts through his mind, his hand tightened around the amber necklace that was currently wrapped around his palm.

He was unsure if it was his own predicament causing his palms to sweat, or if the amber necklace was actually heating up in his hand.

"Amulet?" Elliott asked and found himself again mentally scolding himself for the quaky frightened voice that he spoke with.

"Amulet?" he repeated, with a concerted effort to sound stronger and control the quiver in his voice.

"Elliott, you are the Darach Nua, each Darach Nua is guided by an element. I am Tuath, Guardian of the Watchtower of the North, your powers are elemental, as are mine, and we are guided by the element of earth. The amulet has been waiting for you and when you found it, it called me as your guide. You need to leave this place now. The Darach Nua are waiting to meet you, but when you need me, I will be here. Keep the amulet close to your heart." The tall man waved his hand towards Elliott who was by now dumbstruck and silent. As he did Elliott felt cold metal against his chest. He looked down and the amulet was now around his neck. He looked up and there was nothing in front of him but the tall northern oak tree.

Chapter Seven
Darach Nua

Elliott gathered himself together, collected his equipment and turned to walk down the hill, and then he remembered, Benjy? He called to Benjy but he was nowhere in sight, now he would be in trouble, he was late, wet and he had lost the dog, not to mention he had been inside a tree talking to a 'Guardian?'

Elliott shook his head in disbelief at the morning he had just encountered. He wanted to tell Nanny if anyone would understand she would, but he couldn't, how could he tell anyone, if you hadn't experienced it, how could you possibly believe it?

He could see the stone wall and the gate to the lane between Shin's farm and Nanny's house and he was quite relieved, he felt exhausted. As he approached the wall he could see Benjy laying in the sun beneath the stone sign for the farm. That was a relief one less thing for him to worry about. He slowed down ready to put his bag on the wall, better take a few minutes to collect his thoughts. As he swung his bag up he tripped over a rock embedded in the grass and landed spreadeagled in front of the gate on top of a very disgruntled Benjy. He jumped up rubbing his toe indignantly, he went to kick the offending rock but then thought better of it, although he thought he should move it before old Isabella suffered the same fate. He tried to pull the rock from the entwined thatch that had wrapped itself around it like a woven grass cocoon. As he ripped at the undergrowth to reveal a carved and purposefully shaped stone rather than a crude rock, he rubbed it to remove the overgrowth and realised it had some kind of pattern carved into the stone itself. He pulled down his sleeve and used it to rub the pattern removing years of encrusted dirt and moss, he blew the dust away and sat back to examine it. WIDDER. What did this mean he thought? He dragged the stone to the wall and placed it out of harm's way, this was a question for old Isabella another day, today had much more pressing questions to be mulled over.

"Benjy, let's go! We have cousins to meet." Elliott pulled the gate closed behind him and as he did the thunder rolled deep and heavy overhead. Elliott found himself starting to count out loud to see how far away the lightning was. 'One' the lightning struck, a huge fork lightning and it looked like it was right over Nanny's house. He zipped up his jacket and just in time as it happened as the heavens opened, vertical, powerful storm rain poured from the sky. "Perfect, Benjy, just perfect." Elliott looked at Benjy and couldn't help but smile as Benjy's usual large, hairy persona had been reduced to that of a boney, drowned rat, as the rain soaked through his masses of hair. Together they ran the rest of the way to Nanny's; as they approached the driveway, Elliott could see a strange car with a foreign registration plate. His cousins had arrived. This was not the cool, city welcome Elliott had envisioned.

Elliott burst through the back door into Nanny's kitchen to face an array of startled faces. Nanny was the first to speak. "Elliott! Where have you been? You look like a drowned rat and look at Benjy." As Elliott stood in the kitchen soaking wet with droplets of rain dripping off the end of his nose, he noticed the three unfamiliar faces. He quickly tried to smooth over his sodden hair and wipe the drips from his face. He tried to dry his hands on his saturated jeans and offered his hand out. "Hi, I'm Elliott, a very wet Elliott I'm afraid."

"Hi, I'm Roisin and this is my big little brother, Mark." Roisin beamed her friendliest welcome smile and held her hand out.

Just as Elliott took Roisin's hand to reciprocate, the sky lit up with lightning, thunder roared and the wind howled through the open back door. Nanny quickly closed the door and Mark stood up. He looked older than Elliott when they stood beside each other but it was as Roisin said, he was her big little brother and he stood head and shoulders above both Roisin and Elliott. Mark reached out his hand to say hello to his cousin and as he did fork lightning struck the huge apple tree in Nanny's garden. Everyone jumped up to see what had happened The storm was ferocious and you could see the burnt embers where a branch had been severed from the apple tree.

Nanny spoke to Roisin's mother. "You won't be travelling back to Ireland tonight, Shiona. You better call Irish Ferries and rearrange, you can sleep in my office, the kids will be fine all bunked up in the spare room."

They all stood for a moment looking out of the kitchen window, it was as though they were surrounded by an apocalyptic storm and they were all silent as though hypnotised in the moment.

"Don't fret, my squirrels." Nanny said "It's just a summer storm, it's been brewing for weeks," and with that she started to lay the table. "Come on, which one of you three is going to be my little helper?" Roisin jumped up to accept the challenge and Nanny passed her an apron. "The rest of you can clear out of the kitchen while we put lunch out."

Roisin had always been Nanny's little helper in Ireland, and the fact that Nanny remembered and had kept her mini apron was a familiar feeling she appreciated right now. It may have been three years, but Nanny was still Nanny; without prompting Roisin went over to Nanny and gave her a huge hug, squeezing her arms around her waist. "I love you, Nanny."

"And I love you, my little squirrel, you didn't think a few miles or a little time would ever change that did you?" And with that Nanny gave Roisin one of those smiles, the ones where she just knew what was in her mind, but she couldn't know, could she?

"What's for lunch?" Roisin asked trying to break the moment. She loved Nanny but she couldn't know about the book? She was just being paranoid she had to be she tried to convince herself. "It's a northern delicacy" With that Nanny opened the oven and the smell that filled the kitchen was a mouth-watering mix of stew and pastry, perfect comfort food for a wet day in the stormy weather.

"Pies," Nanny laughed. "You will grow to love them while you are here and if you are really hungry you can have a Wigan Kebab!"

"What's a Wigan kebab?" Roisin asked.

"It's a pie... in a barm cake," laughed Nanny. "Come on, girls, come on, squirrels," Nanny called to the others to come and eat.

Roisin, can you get the pickled cabbage out of the cupboard behind you please?"

Everyone tucked heartily into Nanny's homemade pies with pickled cabbage, homemade pickled cabbage no less. Nanny was a wonder with preserves and if it grew there was a chance at some point Nanny had preserved it.

With lunch finished and the dishes cleared away, Nanny called to Roisin and Mark to get their bags.

"Come on, Elliott, you are practically part of the furniture, you can help me get your cousins settled in and show them where everything is."

With that Nanny led the way upstairs, Mark liked Nanny's stairs they were made of oak and he could fit his arm between each spindle as they made their way up to the guest bedroom.

"Mind you don't get your arm stuck, those spindles are made from an oak tree from Shin's farm, probably hundreds of years old. If you get your arm stuck I'm afraid it's your arm that's coming off!"

Nanny showed them to the guest bedroom, it was situated at the back of the house, with a window almost the length of the room. Mark and Roisin walked straight to the window and looked out, Goderich brook ran close to the perimeter behind Nanny's and beyond that was a field that led into the top paddock, old Isabella would use it for the horses to frolic in.

"Nanny," They both said at the same time and then laughed aloud.

"Jinx," they both said together as was the ritual whenever they both said the same thing at the same time.

"Well, what is it?" Nanny asked smiling; she knew why they were both so impressed.

"The horses," they both said in unison again, "Jinx" and again started to laugh.

"I didn't think you had horses in Manchester, there must be a least a dozen horses," Mark said,

"I didn't think you had farms in Manchester," Roisin said.

"Flippen eck, where do you think we are? On the moon?" Elliott replied. "That's Shin's farm out the back, my friend owns it, old Isabella," Elliott stated quite proudly.

Mark and Roisin looked at each other, could it be a coincidence? "Did you say old Isabella?" Roisin asked.

"Yes she's a lovely old lady, she has had the farm forever and I go and help her whenever I can. I can introduce you if you like you could help with the horses?"

Roisin and Mark looked at each other, it had to be a coincidence, and either that or this day was getting stranger by the hour.

"Roisin, you are in the single on the top bunk, Mark and Elliott you will have to share the double on the bottom I'm afraid, but you can always top and tail if you need your own space."

Nanny pointed to a triple sleeper bunk bed facing the window.

"Half the wardrobe is empty for you to put your belongings in and there is a wash basket behind the door, you are all a bit too big now for me to be picking up after you, if it's in the basket I will wash it if it's on the floor I will presume it's rubbish and put it in the bin. I will leave you to settle in, the remote for the tv is on the window."

As Nanny walked out of the room she turned around as if she had remembered something, "You better get to know each other, we haven't long."

And with that she left the room and closed the door behind her.

"What did Nanny mean, we haven't long?" Roisin asked

"Long until what?" Mark replied,

"I don't know," said Elliott "but this is a very strange day altogether."

"I second that," said Roisin.

"I third it," said Mark.

The three of them then flopped back onto the double bed.

The moment's silence was broken with the sound of an ear shattering barking and snarling coming from downstairs. Elliott sat bolt upright, "Benjy," he shouted followed by Roisin.

"Gypsy," the three cousins all looked at each other for a second before all darting towards the stairs. As they made their way out of the bedroom and down the staircase, the noise from the kitchen was like a pack of wolves had moved in. Roisin was first in line, she was worried Benjy would hurt Gypsy; Gypsy was not an aggressive dog unless she was challenged or Roisin was. As the cousins rounded the bottom of the stairs the scene they encountered was not what they expected; there was no confrontation, no face off with the family dogs, in fact quite the opposite. Benjy and Gypsy were side by side, facing the window, down on their haunches, lips stripped back baring their teeth, but they were not fighting, they were stood side by side against a common enemy, united, but what enemy? Against who? Lightning lit up the sky, thunder rolled through the air, it felt heavy and claustrophobic.

"Here," Roisin called to Gypsy. Gypsy whimpered and came around to stand beside Roisin.

"Benjy," Elliott called and without question Benjy stood between Elliott and Mark.

"What is it, boy?" Elliott rubbed Benjy's head, both dogs heeled immediately that they were called but they were uneasy.

"Come on," said Elliott. "They're not barking for nothing, flippin 'eck, if there is something out there, let's see what it is."

With that Elliott rushed out of the back door, followed swiftly by Roisin and Mark.

"Wait," called Mark, "What do you mean 'something' out there?"

"Mark, I can't explain but I have had the strangest day, you don't know me and I don't you, but things have happened today that don't happen in real life, and I might be losing my mind or there might actually be 'something' out here, are you coming with me or not?"

"Elliott, this day has been filled with things that don't make sense, so I see your weird day and I raise it by 'am I dreaming.' Seriously, Roisin, wait in the house, me and Elliott have this."

"Not a chance my day hasn't exactly been normal either!" With that Roisin chased after the boys into the back garden.

They all stood at the fence at the bottom of Nanny's garden that overlooked Shin's farm. Benjy and Gypsy were stood with them, still barking furiously, you could see the hair on the back of Gypsy's neck standing up. As they looked over the fence the field that had earlier had a dozen or more horses in was now empty except for three, two bay horses and a jet black stallion. It appeared as though the bay horses were trying to prevent the black stallion from approaching the fence, he seemed determined, snorting the air and tossing his mane, but the bay horses were having none of it.

"Hey there, calm down," shouted Elliott.

The horses heard him and stopped instantly, the black stallion reared up aggressively on his back legs causing Gypsy and Benjy to increase the volume and intensity of their barking. The bay horses walked towards the fence and stood there silently with their heads bowed. "What's going on with them?" Roisin asked the boys but they were as surprised as Roisin.

"I have never seen horses act like that," Mark said.

"I have never seen them horses act like that," Elliott added.

The black stallion was now out of sight in the top paddock but the bay horses remained, motionless like statues, still with their heads bowed.

"It must have been old Blacky the dogs didn't like, they have calmed down now he's out of sight," said Mark.

Lightning cracked overhead and the heavens opened. "Come on, get in out of the rain," shouted Roisin.

"I want to know about Elliott's unbelievable day." Elliott stopped dead in the middle of the patio.

"I can tell you, I wasn't going to tell anyone, but for some reason I feel like I need to tell you, but I tell you what, you won't believe me."

Mark and Roisin both smirked.

"After the day we have had, Elliott, we might just believe anything," said Roisin and she walked into the house. "Come on, boys," she called as though self-appointed leader of the new gang.

As the new gang dried themselves off in the kitchen, there was an intense silence, no one spoke but many glances were exchanged.

"What are you three up to?" Shiona asked. "You have only been together for an hour and you are already thick as thieves."

Nanny interrupted before she could interrogate them further. "They are family, they have a natural connection that time and distance can't stop, leave them be they have a lot of catching up to do, go on up, squirrels, I will bring hot chocolate and something sweet, you can stay out of our way in the bedroom while you share your stories."

"But, Nanny, how did you know we were..." Mark couldn't finish his sentence as Roisin interrupted.

"Come on, boys, out from under Nanny's feet," and glared at Mark, the glare that meant shut up and shut up now.

Mark grabbed Roisin by the arm as they crossed the landing. "Why did you make me shut up, I just wanted to know how Nanny knew Elliott was going to tell us about his strange day?"

"Because we didn't tell Nanny, and neither did Elliott. It seems Nanny knows more than she is letting on and until we have worked out what is going on, the less we say to anyone the better, agreed?"

"Agreed."

"Agreed," replied both Mark and Elliott seemingly accepting Roisin as their self-appointed leader.

The three of them walked into the bedroom. "Mark close the door, Elliott close the curtains." Roisin handed out instructions as though this was a military exercise. The boys looked at each other, then at Roisin and decided it was better to do as she said than to bother arguing the point. Roisin went over to the wardrobe where she had placed her backpack and threw it on the bottom bunk.

"Mark, help with the duvet like we do at home."

Mark stepped into action, he knew exactly what she meant. They each took a corner and stripped the duvet back, lifting it up and tucking one of the long edges into the base at the front of the top bunk creating a perfectly private tent.

"Have you still got the mag light Grandad got you?" Roisin asked Mark.

Mark went over to the wardrobe and retrieved his own bag. He started to pull out all manner of strange items, a compass, a fire starter's kit, Swiss army knife and a roll of Gorilla tape.

"Here it is," Mark proudly switched his mini torch between high beam and intermittent flashing, grinning profusely.

"OK, save your battery for now," Roisin instructed. "Nanny will be up shortly with our snacks, we wait until she has been and then it's time to get to the bottom of this day."

As if on cue Nanny knocked on the door. "Snack time squirrels." Nanny walked in with a tray laden with steaming mugs of hot chocolate and marshmallows, chocolate chip cookies and wagon wheels, but there was a lot of wagon wheels.

"I love you, Nanny," Mark said at the delicious sight.

Nanny put the tray on the dresser. She turned to Mark and said, "Don't eat them all at once, put some in your backpack, you never know when you might need an emergency snack and you appear to have most of the basic survival equipment but you won't last long without food." With that she kissed him on the top of the head and gave him a wink.

Nanny closed the door behind her when she left. Roisin stood as still as a statue with her head cocked to one side as though listening. "What are you doing?" Elliott asked.

"Making sure the coast is clear of course. OK, in the tent," said Roisin very matter of factly. Roisin, Mark and Elliott all climbed inside the tent and sat crossed legged on the large bottom bunk, Mark and Elliott looked at Roisin waiting for instructions.

"OK boys, we are going to start with questions. We can each ask each other one question and we have to wait for a full answer before we discuss, then we will decide if something weird is actually going on, deal?"

The boys again looked at each other for conformation and then at Roisin. "Agreed," they both replied and the three of them joined hands to shake on it.

"Deal," they all said in chorus, as they did the room lit up with yet another huge lightning strike and the rain drove hard against the window.

"What is that noise?" Elliott asked, he was feeling uneasy, "Listen." There it was a scratching sound.

Mark laughed. "That's Gypsy, she wants to come in."

Mark jumped up and was out of the tent in a flash, he opened the door and there, just as he had said was Gypsy. Sat beside her was Benjy and as he opened the door Gypsy and Benjy walked into the room in unison as though they were two dogs with one mind. They jumped up onto the bed and entered the tent. Mark followed them and managed to squeeze in-between the two new best friends.

"Let's begin," said Roisin.

Chapter Eight
Who are we?

Roisin carefully and slowly unzipped her bag as though she were performing a medical procedure. she carefully removed the book and placed it in the middle of the three of them whilst they sat crossed legged in the tent.

"Mark, Maglite," Roisin instructed.

Elliott tried to take the book to get a better look. Roisin slapped his hand gently. "Not yet," she said in her best authoritarian voice.

"I will start. My question is to Elliott. Who is old Isabella and how did you meet?"

"That's two questions," said Mark.

"Apologies, who is old Isabella?" Roisin replied and glared at Mark.

"Why are you so interested in old Isabella? I thought we were going to discuss our strange day and I haven't even seen her today?" Elliott asked.

"Trust me if our suspicions are correct all will become clear; somehow I think old Isabella has something to do with us all having a strange day, but it's my question, so please don't ask any more until it's your turn."

Roisin clasped her hands together as she said this and gave Elliott the 'I'm waiting" face'. Elliott looked at Mark. Mark just shook his head, he knew better than to argue when Roisin had that face.

Elliott began, he told them how he had heard of old Isabella long before he met her and that some of the neighbours had said she was a witch, how on that day on their first meeting he had been afraid because of this, but when he actually spoke to her she was a lovely, kind lady who actually wasn't old she just appeared it from a distance and she had needed his help. He told them how he would often go walking with Isabella and how they talked about history and times gone by, plant law and herbal cures and that often he would help with the horses and chores on the farm but he again insisted he hadn't see her today as she was preparing for a visit from her children. He had been out since eight that morning, metal detecting with Benjy, that was how his strange day had started.

"Did you find anything?" piped up Mark.

"Mark, don't waste your question you only have one to begin with." scolded Roisin.

"Well Mark's question would have told you more about my strange day than yours did," replied Elliott who was now starting to get frustrated.

He sat back on his heels and pushed his curly hair behind his ears, a sure sign he was feeling the pressure.

"Be patient, I didn't mean to snap I just need more information before we tell you about our strange day. OK Mark, your turn"

"Why is it Mark's turn next? I'm beginning to get the feeling I'm being interrogated," protested Elliott.

"Because I think you will be far more surprised at our strange day and I am trying to work out if they are connected," said Roisin.

"Mark, your question?"

"Did you find anything?" Mark blurted out without a moment's thought, Roisin glared again at Mark.

"Finally," said Elliott.

"A question that actually relates to my strange day, you better sit back because you are not going to believe what I am about to tell you. In fact I'm not actually sure I believe it myself. I was knocked out for a while so maybe it's not true?"

Elliott looked genuinely confused by his own admission. "When we were outside and the horses were being just, well, weird, I felt then I needed to tell you so, if this is the result of being knocked on the head or not I will tell you."

Elliott started at the beginning, when he had set out with Benjy on his solo adventure. He explained how old Isabella had found a coin and marked the spot for him so he could check if there was any more. He paused, looked at Roisin and Mark and shook his head. "I can't believe I'm telling you this, I wasn't planning on telling anyone, well except old Isabella and then Nanny."

"You're not great at keeping secrets then," Mark said beaming with a slightly sarcastic smile. That broke the awkward silence and Elliott laughed out loud his curls again relaxed and falling into his eyes.

"It's so unbelievable, flippen eck I hardly believe it myself. Well, here goes, I fell into a tree. There I said it."

Roisin and Mark looked at each other.

"Is that it?" Roisin asked looking deflated.

"Not just in a tree like in a hole, and anyway I thought you couldn't interrupt until I finished."

"Sorry."

Roisin looked quite sheepish as she realised she had broken her own rules. "Please continue."

"Well as I said, I fell into a tree, but not just a hole in a tree, when I fell in it was like a tree cave and I wasn't alone."

Elliott paused as though for dramatic effect, looking at his cousin's faces and waiting for their reaction.

"Was Siar there?" Mark asked eagerly.

"Who is Siar? No and no interrupting," Elliott continued. He told them how he had initially thought the tree was talking to him but then how Tuath had come forward and introduced himself. How he had appeared as an old man in long green clothing with disgustingly dirty feet and how Tuath had called him the Darach Nua and that Tuath was his elemental guide. But there he stopped. He did not mention the amulet.

"Now it's my turn," said Elliott.

"But I have questions," interrupted Mark. "About Tuath"

"Mark, not until we have all asked and answered," Roisin reminded him. "Ask away," Roisin replied to Elliott.

"My question is for Mark. Who is Siar?"

"Good question," replied Mark again beaming.

"He is Mo Chara, that means my friend in Irish by the way. Siar is my elemental guide or so he told me in my dream, but I did sort of meet him for a moment when we were on the ferry but that was before my dream where he told me he was my guide, but after my dreams where there were four of them and not just Siar."

"Woooah slow down, Mark, I'm getting confused so is…?"

"No questions." Roisin cut Elliott off and gave Mark the nod to continue. Mark's face was animated as he checked he had a captive audience.

"Well it started in Ireland, I was having trouble sleeping. Every night I would dream about these four fellas in sort of long gowns, it was scaring me a bit and I would wake up sweating and feeling uneasy. Then on the boat I helped an old man who actually wasn't old and he called me Mo Chara and he looked like the men in my dreams. Then I fell asleep, not just randomly, I was laying on a bench by the window, and in my dream Siar, the young old man from my dreams was there. We were running through the forest trying to get away from someone called Silas, and then we were in a really tall round tower where the sound of water was deafening. Siar said he was my guide and his powers were made of water and he needed my help, then I woke up, oh and he said I was Darach Nua too."

Elliott sat back on his heels again, not sulking this time, but he pushed his curls behind his ears and his face was very solemn. He was thinking very hard about what Mark had said trying to understand the connection.

"Elliott, you have one question left," Roisin reminded him.

"I know, I'm just trying to decide what to ask, this is all crazy. I don't know what to ask to get the right answer."

Elliott was very quiet for a moment and then looked at Roisin. "My question is for Roisin, what made your day strange?"

"Good question, Elliott. I was beginning to wonder what you would ask me, mine started last night with this book." As she said it she tapped the book affectionately and they all looked at it. "Widdershins, I started to read it last night in Ireland."

Roisin continued to explain how she had read the story about a small farm in the olden times around Manchester. She explained about the lady named old Isabella who had called the forest folk to a meeting. To protect a stone from someone called Silas.

She went on to explain how when she had taken the book from her bag in the car everything except the writing on the covers had disappeared. "Look for yourself."

With that she passed the book to Elliott, he looked at the front cover, tracing the name with his finger. "Widdershins," he said out loud, his face showing deep concentration. He turned the book over and read the inscription on the back:

To read this book and read it right, you must only read it when the moon is bright. Siar.

"But there were pages and pages of writing last night, I know, I read it." Roisin sounded almost desperate that Elliott believed her.

"I believe you," Elliott said in a gentle voice and touched Roisin's hand, she smiled back. The three of them sat in silence for a moment absorbing what each of the others had said.

"So, Roisin, how did you find out about Siar?" Elliott asked.

"I went to read my book and couldn't believe the pages were blank, I thought Mark was playing a prank on me. When I asked Mark he knew nothing about it, then he saw the inscription on the back and he told me about Siar."

"You two are lucky, I don't know if I would be so close or trusting if I had a brother or sister," said Elliott,

"You don't need to," said Mark, "You have us now," and he gave Elliott the full warmth of his smile.

Roisin spoke up. "When we were in the kitchen and you were talking about old Isabella at Shin's farm, we just couldn't believe it was a coincidence."

Mark opened the book and shone his Maglite on the pages. "Mark," said Elliott. "It says by moon light not Maglite," and with that they all started to laugh. "What does it mean?" asked Elliott.

"If me and Mark are Darach Nua, what are you? And what is Darach Nua?"

They all lay back on the bed thinking about it. Roisin spoke first. "In the book there were four guardians I think you have met one each, and there was old Isabella, who we think you have met, Elliott."

"Agreed," said Mark. "But what is the connection to us, why is this happening?

"Flippen eck!" shouted Elliott as he suddenly stopped laughing and sat bolt upright. "Get dressed I have to show you something."

"We are dressed?" Mark replied.

"No, wellies and stuff we are going out into the storm," replied Elliott already running for the door.

"Come on, Benjy."

Roisin and Mark looked at each other, then both jumped up and went to their suitcases, wellies, coats and hats in hand they ran for the door.

"Come on, Gypsy," as they all ran down the stairs at high speed and high volume. "Hey what's all the commotion?"

Shiona and Kairen stuck their heads out of the living room to see what all the noise was. "Nothing, Mum, we're just taking Benjy out," shouted Elliott.

The three of them dressed as quickly as they could and ran out of the back door, Benjy and Gypsy running alongside of them. As they got to the end of the lane that led to Shin's farm Elliott stopped, he was doubled over with his hands on his knees catching his breath.

"Are you OK?" Roisin asked.

"Yes of course," laughed Elliott breathless and grinning.

"I just wanted to get out before any of them came up with a reason for us not to go out in the storm."

"Not just a pretty face," laughed Roisin.

"That's nothing wait until you see what I have to show you." With that, Elliott marched off ahead with Benjy by his side and his curls blowing in the wind and rain.

"Come on, Mark, let's see what the fuss is about," shouted Roisin. The wind was getting stronger and she had to shout to be heard.

The three cousins headed up Shin's Lane pushing their way through the wind and rain. The dogs were now soaking wet but seemed to be in their element. Benjy up ahead of Elliott and Gypsy at the rear, both running and barking like it was a beautiful summer's day.

"It's here!" shouted Elliott as Roisin and Mark caught up with him, they both looked around but were unsure what it was Elliott was showing them. "The sign," said Elliott as he pointed to the stone sign on the wall. "Shin's Farm."

"I don't get it?" said Mark. "Me neither," said Roisin.

"You will, just wait," said Elliott as he opened the gate.

They all walked through, Elliott closed the gate behind them and then announced proud as punch, "There it is, it meant nothing when I found it, until I saw the book." He bent down and rolled the stone over, wiped the dirt and moss away to reveal the word WIDDER.

"I still don't get it" said Mark.

They all just stared at the stone in silent disbelief, they turned to each other and as if on cue they all said it.

"WIDDERSHINS."

The rain stopped and the clouds cleared, the three cousins stood there, soaking wet, trying to absorb what they were seeing.

"But the book is a legend, just a myth," Roisin said. Mark and Elliott stood there in silence.

"But Darach Nua? Is it real? Are we Darach Nua?" Mark asked his face unusually troubled.

"We need answers but first we need to know the questions," said Elliott. "And I think the person who can give us answers is not too far away."

As he spoke he turned to look at the farmhouse, smoke was winding from the chimney, someone was home and someone needed to answer some questions.

"But," said Mark still looking quizzical, "what if we go there and say, Hey, we are Darach Nua and you are not just old Isabella but really old Isabella, then she doesn't know what we are talking about?"

"To be honest," said Elliott, "Even if she doesn't know what we are talking about, there is no one I would trust more not to think we had all lost our marbles, she, well, she just knows stuff. All the stuff. About everything."

As they walked up the hill towards the farmhouse the three cousins were silent, each of them unsure of what they were about to say and how it would be received.

"Wait," said Roisin, again assuming her role as leader. "Can we just decide what exactly we are going to say, after all, Elliott, not only are we going to an old lady's house unannounced, we are about to tell her some bat crazy stuff, and well, we don't want to scare her, and, we have never met her or her us."

"Exactly, what Roisin said," Mark added and then put his hands in his pockets and started to kick the grass, clearly uncomfortable at the entire scenario.

Elliott reached up and put his arm around Mark's shoulder. "Don't worry, pal, old Isabella is very cool, if she thinks we are crazy she will tell us, but if she does, I'm pretty sure she will have an explanation for us as to what's actually going on. Roisin, you say you don't know her, or her you, but I have been talking about you two arriving for the whole summer. She knows you as well as I do and she loves Ireland. She said she had friends called O'Neill in the old times, trust me, it will be fine."

"Yeah how long ago in the old times?" Mark asked.

Elliott and Roisin both looked at Mark when he made this remark, but no one replied, they both nodded as though to agree that actually, they did not know when the 'old times,' actually were any more. Last week? Last year or last century?

They reached the path that led to the back door of the farmhouse. It was a broken stone path with bits of grass and weeds growing between the cracks, well-worn stones that looked like they could have been there for a hundred years.

"Elliott," Roisin touched Elliott on the elbow. "Wait, I'm not at all sure about this."

"Trust me please, both of you, I know old Isabella well enough for the three of us, this is the right thing to do. In fact I have never felt surer of anything. I feel like I have to tell her, even if you turn around and go back to Nanny's right now, I'm still going to knock on the door and tell her about our strange day."

Elliott took a step forward and raised his hand to knock on the door. "Wait." Again Roisin grabbed Elliott's elbow. "If we are doing this we do it together, agreed?" She held out her hand palm down, "We are in this together."

Mark and Elliott each placed their hands on top of Roisin's, first Elliott then Mark.

"Agreed."

They stood shoulder to shoulder and knocked on the door, three hands knocking in unison, and then they waited.

Old Isabella heard the knock on the door and as she did, the pages of her book fluttered open to a new page. Isabella left the room at the back of her kitchen and drew the heavy red curtain closed. She could make out three shadowy figures through the glass on the door. As she opened the door she saw Elliott in the middle flanked by two very scared looking faces.

Isabella quickly studied the female face to Elliott's left, the face she recognised in her memory. She turned to look at the boy, a strong warm looking face filled with kindness, he was a true O'Neill she thought.

"Isabella, I'd like to introduce my cousins."

Old Isabella was silent for a moment studying the three cousins standing uncomfortably silent on her doorstep,

"I…" Elliott started to speak but old Isabella held up her hand to stop him.

Elliott stopped talking instantly as though her command had indeed silenced him. Isabella wiped her hands on her apron and stood back. As she opened the door to the farmhouse she spoke softly, "I have been waiting such a long time for this day."

She closed the door behind them, turned to face them all, and held out her hands, "Welcome, Darach Nua."

Chapter Nine
Lessons from the past

Roisin, Mark and Elliott stood in shocked silence staring at old Isabella, then they looked at each other, their disbelief was clear to see, both to each other and to old Isabella.

"Elliott, make some tea, we had better loosen your tongues if we are to prepare a plan before the solstice."

Elliott stared at his cousins and slowly walked over to the range to collect the old copper kettle and carried it slowly to the sink, not speaking and not taking his eyes off his cousins.

"Isabella…" Elliott turned around to speak but Isabella raised her hand again to signal silence.

"Hold your questions for the moment, let's take tea and I will tell you all a story from long ago, but listen well, there are lessons to be learned from the past."

The cousins each exchanged glances; they could not believe what they were hearing.

Roisin and Mark had been worried that old Isabella would think they were crazy or tell their parents they had been making up stories, but none of them had thought even for a moment that old Isabella had been waiting for them, or that she actually knew what was going on with this strangest of days.

"Don't just stand there like oaks rooted to the ground, come sit around the fire, let's see what the flames would like you to know."

Old Isabella reached into her apron pocket and when she withdrew her hand she had three green vials each labelled 718.

"I'm not drinking that," Mark said and stood up and stepped away from the fireside knocking over a bucket of sticks as he did.

"Indeed you are not," replied old Isabella quite shocked. "You cannot drink this until after your ceremony, the magic would be too strong. I would never know which time to find you in, or even where to start looking."

With that, she laughed as if she had made a joke that only she understood.

"You have one vial each; I will mind it for you until it is needed, but for now a little help along the way will be no harm and it will help you see clearly through the flames. You don't have your powers yet and you need all the help you can get; take the bottle in your right hand and break the wax seal, dab a little on your left wrist and repeat after me."

Mark stepped back towards the fire to his allotted stool, stared at Roisin. Roisin was unsure also, and stared at Elliott.

"How much stranger can today get?" he said to them both with a nervous laugh and started to break the seal around the top of the small green bottle.

"To fix the present the past we must heal."

Old Isabella waited and looked at the cousins for their response. Roisin nudged Elliott as if to prompt him, just as she did, Mark, who was sat on Elliott's other side also nudged him. "Hey I will drop my bottle at this rate," he protested. "Lose your bottle you mean," replied Mark.

Old Isabella coughed and looked sternly at the three of them. "Shall we begin?"

The three cousins now sat side by side on the stools in front of the old fire, Roisin, Elliott and then Mark; they all nodded in silent obedience.

"To fix the present the past we must heal, Lift the veil so the truth will reveal.

"Repair the damage, the wounds in time.

"Return the balance so the guardians can align."

Roisin, Mark and Elliott all repeated the words as old Isabella instructed. She stood up without warning and threw a handful of thyme from her apron onto the open fire. The sparks crackled and the flames changed colour as though they were watching a movie with a frame of flames. As they stared dreamily into the fire, the flames parted and a clearing could be seen, in what appeared to be a forest.

"Watch the flames and the tale will tell, watch the flames and understand well." Isabella murmured the words into the flames. As the three cousins stared into the fire, the room seemed to melt away and the picture in the flames became clear.

Through a clearing in the trees, they could see a boy of around thirteen. He had thick black curly hair and a pale complexion. He appeared to be hiding, hiding and watching. Up ahead chatter and laughter could be heard and it became clear that boy was watching two older children of around fifteen; there was a boy and a girl both with bright red fiery hair and milky complexions, they appeared to be twins.

The red-haired boy stood still as a rock and closed his eyes, there was total silence and the black haired boy was trying to get a better view peering over the rock he was hiding behind.

"Squawk!"

A large black crow flew into the clearing and landed at the feet of the flame-haired twins. It walked around in the dust, in and around them, cocking his head to one side looking at them inquisitively, and as suddenly as he arrived he flew away, his beautiful glossy black wings catching the light. As the crow flew away the flame-haired boy fell to the ground. His companion did not look at all worried and simply sat on a small patch of grass beside him, appearing to be waiting.

The black-haired boy was staring intently not making sound. As the flame-haired boy started to stir his companion went over to him, he sat up slowly as though waking from an afternoon nap. When he sat up he stretched his arms and a beaming smile took over his face.

"What did you see?" his companion asked.

"Not what," he replied, "But who?" again beaming with enthusiasm. "Give me your hands and see for yourself."

With that he took her hands and placed them on his temples. As he did she began to smile, "Can you see it?"

"I can, I can," With that he removed her hands from his temple. "And who did we see?"

In perfect chorus, they both shouted out at the same time, "Silas!"

They jumped up from their seating position and ran over to the rock where the black-haired boy was hiding. "Silas, how many times have we told you not to spy on us? You have your own powers now, why do you insist on sneaking around? You should join us, we could try and draw out your power too."

The older boy spoke affectionately to the black-haired boy but the boy seemed angry. "Why would I want to share my powers with you two, you are Darach Nua and you choose to see the world through a lowly crow's eyes," Silas shouted.

"And you are no better." He turned to the flame-haired girl. "You can see the memories of men and you choose to see his memories of seeing through the eyes of a crow? Why do you waste your powers? Why would you think I want to waste mine with you?"

Silas started to storm away but then turned around angrily. "And as for helping me to draw out my powers, I don't need your help."

With that he reached into his pocket and withdrew a clenched fist. He threw the contents of his fist, a concoction of what looked like powdery herbs at the twins and as it hit the ground it burst into flames. They jumped back quickly but it was too late, the flames caught the bottom of the girl's dress.

"Rowan!" shouted her twin, pushing her to the ground and smothering the flames, but it was too late she was injured, the fabric had melted to her ankle and the skin was blistered and broken. Her brother was afraid to try and remove the melted fabric from the wound as she cried out in pain.

He picked up his sister and hurriedly carried her away into the clearing, soothing her cries as he did.

"Silas, you have gone too far this time. Mother will find out about this."

"Tell Mother if you like, you were always her favourite, Sean, she wouldn't notice if I never returned."

"Silas, don't be so selfish, we are the Darach Nua our strength is increased by each other, we will be together always. Come with me, Rowan is injured and she needs Mother's help, run ahead and tell her to prepare a burn tincture"

Silas looked so angry he might explode, his once pale complexion was reddening by the second and his eyes glared. "You have been the Darach Nua for two years longer than I, and you still need to run to Mother, when will you realise we are each as powerful as she!"

Silas stormed over to his brother Sean. He looked around and snatched a comfrey leaf from the ground and placed it over the burn. He then placed one hand on the ground, it appeared as though he drew power from the earth as he muttered words that the twins could not hear. For a second his eyes were black, he stood again, visibly shaken. "Her burn will heal with no scar, dress it with elderflowers for three days," he snapped and stormed off.

"Silas, you are forbidden from drawing power from the underworld. You know the rules," Sean called after Silas.

Silas turned to look at his brother, his eyes were a darker green now, almost black.

"Have you not realised yet, my brother, for me there are no rules, one day you will see." Sean looked at Rowan's ankle, and what Silas had said was true, it was little more than a graze.

"Sean, we must tell Mother, he is becoming dangerous." Rowan spoke softly, Sean put her down to see if she could take her own weight. She was fine to walk and the only lasting damage was to her dress and her pride,

"I know, little sister, but it will break Mother's heart, I will try to speak to him tonight, it is the solstice and his spirits should be lifted."

"Hardly, little sister, if you don't mind, you are only two minutes older," laughed Rowan. As they walked away into the clearing, the flames closed on the tale from the past.

Old Isabella pushed back her stool and stood up, the scraping sound of the wooden legs on the stone floor brought the three cousins back into the now.

She held out her hand towards the three of them, they looked up in confusion. "Vials please."

They each passed their small green bottle back to old Isabella who promptly deposited them in her apron pocket. "I will mind these, for now. Now I am sure you have many questions, we can talk for a while, but not for long. Your parents will be worried and the dogs are getting restless, although I suspect it's more to do with what they know is coming than the time of day."

Isabella moved to the dining table and sat down; it was a very large table, with four large chairs oddly placed at each corner. There were also four regular chairs placed randomly around the table. Old Isabella signalled for them to sit down by waving her hand at the table, the cousins got up to move over to the table. Mark was about to pull out one of the large corner chairs, Isabella instantly raised her hand to stop him as easily as she had stopped Elliott talking, "You may be a Darach Nua, Mark O'Neill, but you cannot sit in the place of a guardian, not yet at least." And with that she gave Mark a warming smile. Mark gingerly let go of the large chair and seated himself beside it in a very comfortable cushioned dining chair.

Elliott and Roisin, learning quickly from Mark's oversight, sat themselves quietly in two of the other dining chairs. Old Isabella placed herself at the head of the table in a chair as equally large as the four corner guardian's chairs. Old Isabella's chair had a homemade shawl over the back in knitted patchwork squares of green, red, purple and orange and a huge padded cushion to sit on made from the tiniest pieces of patchwork. Each square no more than 3cm wide and delicate embroidery around each tiny piece, the detail was breathtaking.

"Elliott, fetch the tea please. Mark, you are the tallest, take down four of my best Royal Worcester tea cups and saucers from the top shelf of the dresser by the window. Roisin, the milk jug from the pantry please. There is a tin of brownies in the pantry beside the milk, you better get those too. I don't want the Darach Nua passing out with hunger on day one." Old Isabella again laughed as though she had made a private joke.

Old Isabella poured the tea and passed around the beautiful teacups each on their own saucer with a silver spoon nestled between the tea cup and the saucer. She placed the brownies on a matching tiered cake stand in the centre of the table. The whole scene was that of a cosy tea party that you would see in many a fairy tale. As the cousins added their sugar and milk, each took a brownie from the cake stand. Old Isabella reached over and lit the large red pillar candle in the centre of the table, it was only then that Elliott looked around startled, "You have no electric?"

"Very observant, my boy, how many times have you been here over the last three years and today with so many other things to distract you notice this?"

"Well I have always been here during the day."

"Is it not during the day now?" old Isabella asked smiling.

"Yes it is, but, well, it's as though I am seeing *here* for the first time. I don't think I ever really paid attention before, I was so interested in the history of the bricks I never looked at the home."

"Your eyes will see things and notice things that they never noticed before, your ears will hear sounds that only you hear, you will feel the hum of the earth."

Old Isabella smiled so warmly that Roisin swore she could feel the warmth on her own face. "I have felt the hum of the earth before."

"I know, Roisin, our crow told me, beside the oak tree," and old Isabella winked at Roisin, and for a moment, just a fleeting moment she reminded Roisin of Nanny.

They all sipped their tea very quietly, peering over the edge of the tea cups at each other, waiting for someone to speak.

Finally Roisin regained her composure and decided to resume her role as unappointed leader. "Old Isabella, sorry I mean Isabella." Roisin's face flushed at her mistake, Isabella laughed aloud, a truly hearty belly laugh.

"I know that is what people call me, they have for more years than I care to count. I was once young and my mother was old Isabella; but for the longest time, I have been old Isabella. You, my dears, can call me simply Isabella."

"I'm, I'm, I'm, sorry," stammered Roisin, still flushed from embarrassment.

"Isabella, who are you, and who are we, and what is going on?"

"Exactly," said Elliott finding his voice, "How can we have been friends for so long and yet you never once mentioned anything to me." Elliott looked quite perturbed as he asked this.

"Elliott, we have been friends now for several years, I thought, no, I hoped, that first day when we met beside the tree when you helped me, but I thought it wasn't possible as you were an only child. It was only when you told me of your cousins, I knew it may be possible, and when you told me they were O'Neills from Ireland I was sure. A great Clan from the old times that I knew and trusted very well."

Isabella placed her hand on Elliott's hand as a sign of comfort and friendship and smiled. He smiled back and he meant it, it wasn't an empty placating smile, he really did care for Isabella and somehow he had known, when they needed help, this was where they needed to come.

"What do you want from us?" Mark finally spoke up and his expression was still one of disbelief and mistrust. It was an expression that you didn't see often on Mark's face as he always gave everyone the benefit of the doubt but he had moved his chair closer to Roisin and he was clearly looking out for his sister.

"Mark O'Neill, it's unlike your character to be so mistrusting, open your eyes and your heart as you did to Siar, I am here to help you not harm you."

Isabella stood up and reached over the table to touch Mark's hand. Isabella smiled at Mark and as she did his shoulders dropped and he started to relax.

"My Darach Nua, do you know what this means?" Isabella asked.

Mark stood up from his chair. "New oaks," he beamed as he said it, " I actually don't know why as I never paid attention before but when Siar speaks to me in Gaelic, I understand every word."

"It's your heritage that is why, you are correct Darach Nua is new oak, in time you will meet the Darach Sean, the old oak, these were the Darach Nua before you, before Silas, well, before Silas changed and none have been since."

Isabella looked sad as she said this and looked to the floor. Elliott reached over and touched her hand as she had his, as he did she looked up and smiled but the three cousins could see the shine in her eyes as though she were holding back the tears.

"The time has come, your time to try and rebalance the past and recover the stones. Tonight you must read the book, it will guide you, you will have many guides, some you have known for a life time and others you are yet to meet but for today know this, you are Darach Nua. You will receive your powers on the solstice in three days. I cannot instruct you or offer you the answers, but I can also never lie to you. I am the Keeper of Time and I will protect you with my life."

Chapter Ten
The key

As the cousins made their way down the hill towards Nanny's house, they had much to talk about and yet not one of them spoke. They silently trudged through the damp grass until they reached the gate. Mark went over to the stone that Elliott had revealed earlier in the day. Although it seemed like a lifetime ago now, despite it only being a few hours.

"We didn't ask Isabella about Widdershins," Mark said as he turned to his cousins.

Elliott nodded in agreement and pushed his curls away from his face. "In fact," said Elliott, "there are lots of things we didn't ask Isabella about. It feels strange just calling her Isabella after all this time, but if that's what she has asked us to do we should respect it, what did she say was, the Time Keeper? Will she be timing us to do whatever it is we have to do on the solstice? And, what exactly do we have to do on the solstice, and flippen eck! What are our powers, these gifts?"

"She said she was the Keeper of Time not the Time Keeper," said Roisin. "I think there is a difference, and was it just me or did the mighty scary Silas seem a bit weak to you? I was expecting some deadly, dark, seven foot man, possibly with two heads from the way the book and Mark spoke about him." Roisin stood waiting for a response with her hands on her hips, deep in thought.

"I get the feeling," said Elliott, "that we only saw a snapshot of who Silas is, or was. I get the feeling, that he was young there, and there is worse to come."

Elliott turned to Mark who was dragging the name stone onto the wall. "You are very quiet cousin, what are you doing?"

"This is Widdershins. It should have its full title. It's not Shin's farm its Widdershins. There is so much we don't know, we may as well accept what we do know."

He looked to his cousins for agreement. "Agreed," Roisin and Elliott replied.

"I wonder how long that stone has lay in the grass, I wonder when people forgot its full name and started to think it really was called just Shins?" Elliott asked.

His mind was now racing with all his unanswered questions, "And did you see the number of the bottle vial things? 718? Was that a year number or a batch number? I need to make a list of questions, for the next time we see Isabella."

Elliott checked his pockets and was annoyed with himself that he was so unprepared and could not take notes.

"Maybe the book will answer some of our questions this evening; will the moon be full tonight?" asked Mark.

"I don't think it needs to be full, Mark. Just moonlight or we would only be able to read it once a month," replied Elliott.

"We can check on the laptop when we get back, Nanny has a book that tells you the lunar cycles etc. We could also check that other book, an Almanac I think it's called."

"Come on, you two," called Roisin. "We need to get back to the house and get organised before it goes dark, at least the storm's passed so the sky should be clear tonight. One thing I still don't know and I wanted to ask Isabella, but I was afraid. Am I Darach Nua too? I haven't seen a guardian?"

The three cousins stared at each other for a moment. Elliott was first to speak. "Well, when she welcomed us, she referred to us all as Darach Nua, and again when we spoke at the table, and in the fire, there were two boys and one girl, three of them, so I think so, maybe you will meet him soon? Or maybe you don't need one?" replied Elliott.

"I think you are Boss of the Darach Nua," said Mark sarcastically but teaming it with his warmest smile so no offence was taken, they all laughed and set off for Nanny's.

Everyone was gathered in the kitchen as they entered Nanny's house through the back door, discussing the wrath of the storm from earlier and now the bright blue sky. There was a wine bottle in the middle of the table and Nanny looked in her element. Clearly enjoying having all three daughters together, Auntie Jessica and Uncle Aaron had arrived and Flossy the dog, although she resembled a dandelion clock more than she resembled a dog; short legs and a short body with fluffy wispy hair, a Pom and a Yorkshire terrier cross Aunty Jess said, but Shiona said she was a Porky. Kairen thought this was hilarious and they were all laughing and paid little attention to the cousins as they made their way through the kitchen with Gypsy and Benjy in tow.

"Take turns in the shower please, we will be eating in an hour so you can get straight into your PJs. Where have you three been for the last few hours?" asked Nanny.

"We called over to say hello to Isabella," replied Elliott.

"Did she get younger?" asked Nanny. "She was old Isabella when you left."

With that she laughed and shooed the cousins up the stairs. The cousins exchanged silent glances as they headed up the stairs, Nanny did not miss a thing. They threw their bags into the corner of the room. Gypsy and Benjy both lay at the foot of the bottom bunk and started to sleep.

"Look at the pair of them," said Mark. "Some guard dogs they are, they have only been for a walk up the field and they are exhausted." The three of them laughed at this.

"Maybe we should get Flossy up here to guard us while they sleep," joked Elliott and the cousins burst into laughter.

The cousins all took turns getting showered as instructed, into their pyjamas and then went down to join the family for dinner.

"Nanny, do you still have the book about the weather and the moon, I think it was an Almanac?" Elliott asked Nanny as casually as he could.

"What a silly question, Elliott, when have you ever known your nanny to throw a book away before? Of course I still have it but it's not really about the weather." Nanny gave one of her all-knowing smiles. "It's on the top shelf in my office. It's called the Witches Date book. I got it from Isabella for Christmas. It's more to help with gardening with the cycles of the moon and harvest. You can read it but make sure it goes back where you found it, there are many interesting books on that shelf but don't go scaring yourselves reading things you don't understand, some are historical but some are only myths and legends. It's hard to separate fact from fiction at times and please use a bookmark, you know I hate the corners being folded."

"Thank you, Nanny, may we be excused?"

With that Elliott stood up and signalled a look to his cousins to follow. Mark and Roisin immediately followed his lead standing up at the table.

"Of course you may, what polite grandchildren we have raised."

Nanny smiled, and the three cousins and the three dogs, headed upstairs.

"Look, Mark," called Roisin as she pointed to the newest member of the group. "I think Flossy must have heard us earlier." Flossy now trotted obediently behind Gypsy and Benjy.

"Well," said Mark smirking, "You know what Grandad says, "It's not about the size of the dog in the fight but the size of the fight in the dog."

Nanny's office was quite small. It was an office, of that there was no doubt, but it was also a single box room that Grandad had converted for Nanny. She had a captain's desk on one wall with drawers either side and a huge red leather chair that swivelled full circle which was pushed up against it. Beside that was an old Victorian school cupboard that you could see was bursting at the seams; all the other walls were fitted with thick pine shelves from floor to ceiling. Nanny had only been back in England for three years and already the shelves were bursting with books and curiositie's; the strangest looking figurines of what appeared to be gargoyles and even a crystal ball. There was little wall space but the space there was had pictures and paintings hung on the walls and the side of the Victorian cupboard was covered in what looked like home printed photographs of the three cousins at varying ages.

Roisin stood in the centre of the room and commented, "This is a room I would expect Isabella to have, not Nanny." Elliott and Mark both nodded in agreement.

"Where is the book, Elliott?" asked Roisin.

"Up there," pointed Elliott. He pointed to the top shelf that was full of odd sounding books about pagan mythology, herbal law and even a Spell Encyclopaedia. "Let me," said Mark. "You won't be able to reach it."

Mark stepped on the second shelf from the floor, stretched to reach the top shelf, and took down the Date book they were looking for. "Mark, get the Spell Encyclopaedia as well," requested Roisin.

Mark reached out for the large book and just managed to hold his balance as he lifted the huge book down. They took the books and headed off to get settled in the back bedroom in their tent.

"What time is it now?" asked Roisin.

"Seven thirty," replied Elliott. "We still have a few hours before it goes dark, let's see what we can find out before then. Let me get a notebook and pen. Mark, do you think you can hold my weight if I sit on your shoulders?"

"Of course," said Mark, surprised that Elliott would even question his strength. "But why?"

"I just want to check the top shelf in case there is any other book that might give us some clues."

"Good idea," said Roisin. "Mark can easily lift you, Elliott, just be careful." Mark came back with his arms full of books.

"I thought you were looking for '*a*' book, not all the books" said Roisin when she saw that Elliott also had his arms full. "Will Nanny mind you taking all those books down? And what exactly are they about?" Roisin asked Elliott.

Her eyes were wide with shock as the two boys deposited at least five books each into piles at the end of the bunk bed.

"Not at all," said Elliott. "Nanny says the only thing worse than damaging a book is not reading it, and we have a bit of a mixture to be honest, everything from the power of crystals, to paganism and the old religion and Celtic legends. Let's be honest, we have no clue what is going on or what we need to find out about. Nanny has read all these books and I think if Nanny thinks a book is a pile of rubbish she tells me to take it to Tesco to donate to the charity table, so these must have made it through her quality control."

Roisin stopped in her tracks and thought for a moment, "Agreed," she said finally. "She did the same in Ireland and sent the books full of lies as she called them to the charity shop. I'm starting with this one."

It was the Encyclopaedia of 5000 spells. She liked the cover and it was a big thickset book in cream with oldie world pictures of plants and herbs on the cover. As she turned the pages the third page in was a black page, with a warning written in white:

Mark looked over Roisin's shoulder. "You better put that one back, it's not suitable for children," he laughed.

Roisin scowled at him but his big smile made her see the funny side. "I think it means *normal* children," she said smiling, "not Darach Nua."

"You might have a point," Mark said conceding victory.

"What exactly are you looking for?" Roisin wasn't sure if he was asking because he wanted to know exactly what she was looking for, or if he was trying to avoid having to pick a book and do some research, she knew how he hated to study.

"Come sit with me, little brother, we can look together, you always see more when I'm reading."

Mark didn't hesitate at the invitation and jumped on the bottom bunk beside his sister, now he was interested. He didn't mind shoulder surfing but these books were pretty intense and he didn't want the responsibility of missing a vital clue, that is, if any were to be found.

"What are you starting with, Elliott? There is room up here for a little one," joked Mark. "Hey! Less of the little one, you may be taller but I'm older," laughed Elliott jumping on the bed beside the new study group.

"I think I'm going to start with this one The Wheel of the Year. It's all about Sabbats and moon phases and has a section in about the solstice, seeing as though we are getting our powers on the solstice it might be a good place to start. Did you know the Summer Solstice is the longest day of the year and the shortest night?" Elliott asked.

"Something tells me solstice or not, it's going to be our longest day of the year anyway," said Mark. "Do we know if we have to wait until it's dark to get our powers or do we get them on the day? And, really, have you thought about this? What are our powers, we haven't even talked about this, do we have to take them whatever they are? What if we get a bad power like the guy in the skittles advert? I don't want to taste the rainbow."

Mark was grinning now, obviously losing his track of thought and imagining powers of all kinds, each as inappropriate as the last.

"What would you pick if you could have any power?" Mark looked to his cousins for their input,

"What would you choose, Mark? You have clearly given this more thought than we have," asked Elliott.

"Invisibility," Mark said with almost certainty, "Or, super human strength like the Hulk." Mark let out his best Hulk roar, Roisin and Elliott were in stiches of laughter.

"I'm not sure after what we saw in the flames today, that they will be in the list of possibilities," replied Elliott still laughing. "But, if we could choose, I think I would choose flight, to be able to soar like an eagle, Roisin what would yours be?"

"Well," replied Roisin, clearly giving the matter much thought, "I agree with Elliott. I think any powers we get would be sympathetic to nature and given the lack of contact I have had with a guardian, I will probably end up with the power of great gardening! But, if I could choose, I would love to be able to communicate with animals."

"This no guardian thing has really bothered you hasn't it?" asked Elliott.

Roisin looked to the floor sheepishly. "It's just that, well, I kind of feel like I am involved but fraudulently, the guardians have clearly contacted you two and asked for your help, but what contact has been made with me? Nothing."

"Are you crazy, Roisin?" Mark almost shouted he was so surprised at how Roisin felt. "You have the book, the key, the thing we are all sitting around waiting to read so we can see what's actually going on..."

"Or has gone on," interrupted Elliott. "Roisin, I agree with Mark, you have the key because you are the key."

Roisin smiled, her heart was warmed by what Elliott and Mark had said; she placed her hand on the book affectionately and stroked the cover, as she did her expression changed.

"What is it?" asked Mark, "Are you OK?"

Roisin's face had lost the warmth it had shown a moment before and her face had gone pale. "The book is humming, I can feel it, put your hands on mine."

Mark and Elliott quickly put their hands on top of Roisin's and they could feel it, a warmth and a vibration passing through Roisin's hand into their own.

Mark pulled his hand away quickly. "What is that?"

Roisin removed her hand and only Elliott's remained on the book. "It's stopped now," said Elliott.

Mark placed his hand back on top of Elliott's. "Good, that was just weird."

Roisin placed her hand on the book again to check what her cousins had said and the hum returned.

"It's you," said Mark. "It's not the book at all, you are humming Roisin."

Roisin removed her hand and held out a hand to each of them, they all joined hands, but nothing.

"Put your hands back on the book, Roisin, quickly." said Elliott.

Without delay Roisin placed the palms of her hands flat onto the cover of the book, "Mark, touch Roisin's hand," instructed Elliott.

Mark and Elliott both placed a hand onto Roisin's outstretched hands and there it was, the hum, the vibration.

"Roisin," said Elliott, "I think you have found your guide or guardian or whatever it is, you are somehow linked to the book."

The cousins sat in silence looking at each other, then the book, then each other, the feeling through Roisin's hands, through the book was undeniable, the hum was there.

"Boys," said Roisin, "I think it's time to see what the book has to say," Roisin opened the cover, and there as it had been before was a verse:

Read this book and read it well,
Past secrets, it is waiting to tell,
For you it was written, one of three,
The one who's been resting, beside the oak tree,
The curse that was placed, thirteen hundred years and no more,
Is waiting to be lifted, if you open the door.
Things that were there, remain to be found,
Changed only in vision but not in sound.
If you listen, you will hear them - if you listen true
For they are talking - but only to you.
On the thirteenth solstice of their thirteenth summer, the sun will set,

Then the blood moon will eclipse the sun, and out of the darkness the light you will get,

Three that were no more will be again and three that are new will go widdershins.

"There it is again, the name," said Elliott. "So is it not a place?"

He quickly took out his notebook and wrote down the word Widdershins followed by a question mark and underlined it.

"Go on, Roisin, read it to us," said Mark,

Roisin turned the page. "It's different this time, this isn't the story I read, it was about Isabella and a farmhouse in the woods before," Roisin said with a puzzled look on her face.

"It doesn't matter," said Elliott. "Read what's on the page and read it quickly, but don't rush we want to be sure we get it and we understand, but we don't know how long this story will stay the same."

"OK, just don't rush me."

Roisin took a deep breath and prepared to read.

Silas sat alone in his dwelling, you could not call it a home because there were no comforts to be had, it was to all intents and purposes a dwelling and no more, an unused cave, a hollow sunken into a hill. It was dark and damp and seemed to peter off in the distance down a dark and dingy tunnel; it was just as he liked it. There were no people here to bother him, no Dall to diminish the value of his power and most of all, no Darach Nua, to try to smother him with love or kindness and try to bring him back to his true path. As Silas thought of the Darach Nua, his siblings, his face creased with discomfort, such weaklings, such a waste of potential greatness, he was actually doing them a favour by removing what remained of the great power, taking it from them so they could lead their meaningless lives without distraction. Allowing him to move onto greater things, when he became the one and only Darach Nua, things would change.

Silas had struggled with his gift from the day it had been bestowed upon him, from the very night of his celebration. He had received the gift of Herbal Law, to know and understand all plants and to use them as medicine to heal humankind.

87

"Oh my God," Roisin interjected. "He actually got the power of great gardening! I was only joking when I said it earlier."

"Roisin, you need to focus, keep reading," said Elliott very sternly. "We don't have much time."

"Sorry, that just surprised me I expected him to breathe fire or something." Roisin continued to read the words in the book.

Silas had been bestowed with the one gift he already had, he had spent years learning the Herbal Law and plant history to assist him with his future gift, whatever that gift may be, in fact he thought he knew more before he had his powers than when they were bestowed on him, this had left Silas very bitter.

From the day Silas had watched his siblings, Sean and Rowan receive their powers he had wanted to have the power himself. To truly use them, teach the Dall, the blind unbelievers what magic really was. After all, it was partly their fault that he and his kind now had to hide out in the forest and hide their powers. The non-believers were afraid of what they no longer understood. Why was Silas, the only one who cared enough to desire the power, not entrusted to use them fully? All of them.

Since that day, he had planned, and plotted each day becoming closer and closer to taking the powers from Sean and Rowan, his plans were now coming to fruition, before he could claim the powers he had to claim the stones. The solstice stones were the source of the natural power for the Darach Nua and the source of magic in the world, six in total on Island of Angle, he would start with these, but he would need all six to wipe the Darach Nua from the Earth.

It was a new moon tonight, the perfect time for new beginnings. He had made an incantation, created from the foul smelling plants of the bog and the acrid bones of animals passed, tonight he would call the coldness from the earth and thank the Underworld for his new powers, the time had come to destroy the Darach Nua.

Chapter Eleven
Silas — The dark days

Silas had been nurturing his garden around his cave for many years.

The cave had originally been nothing more than a place to store his equipment or spend a moment in quiet contemplation, but as he distanced himself from his people and his family, he would spend more and more time there, alone in his darkness and his thoughts.

The cold, damp, darkness of his dwelling was in stark contrast to the floral abundance of his garden and the fruits and flowers he tended there. Long before Silas had received his gift, he had made the decision to learn all that had been written and to teach himself all the natural magic of the land. For him and his people, this was Herbal Law.

It had been written, that no ill or ailment caused by nature did not have a natural antidote created in equality by the same nature, the good and bad of all things balanced in the truth of the nature of the world.

He had started his own garden when he was around eleven. He tended, with his mother's help, the best of all the plant and herbal varieties known in the magical world, now, many years later, it was a garden that would be the envy of any herbalist, He even thought that secretly his mother envied the magikal store that his garden had become.

The wise man or woman of the village, if he or she had studied well, could cure most ailments with nothing more than a well-tended garden.

In this time Silas's mother was the most skilled in Herbal Law for miles around. She was a Hedge witch, the mother of the Darach Nua, not only could she cure your ails with plants and herbs, but she could call upon nature to enhance her spells, her magic was natural but it was strong not only to cure but to prevent, protect and enhance the lives of the villagers, the Forest people that followed the Darach Nua.

When Silas was young he had watched his mother prepare potions and concoctions, call the Quarters to her circle and had been in awe of her gift, but now he despised her as much as he did his siblings.

Her rules were too strict, she followed the guidance of the Guardians of the Quarters to the letter, never having ambition to change things and refusing to show him how to master the magic of the stones.

The stones were the source of his mother's powers, the source of the Darach Nua and his mother protected them as if they were her own.

This in itself angered Silas, he was the Darach Nua, as far as he was concerned he out ranked his mother in the world of magic and he should be allowed access to the stones to utilise their power fully. He could bring about change and bring sight back to the Dall, he would show them, open their eyes and it would be they who hid in the forest instead of the followers of the Darach Nua, the forest folk.

His mother had insisted this was not the way to bring about change, free will was the right of all humankind and you could not force them to see what their eyes were closed to.

The guardians had warned Silas many times, that he must only follow the true path and that self-ambition could not be a part of his life as long as he was Darach Nua. He must be selfless always, putting the balance of the natural world and the wellbeing of his people above the selfish desires he held for himself. Silas did not think his desires were selfish, they were just all too blind to see exactly what he could offer the world, under his guidance.

In his mind's eye, his plans were clear; he would take the stones, one by one, building his strength. The forest folk, his mother, his siblings would not even know what was happening until it was too late, until the only stone that remained was theirs, and whilst strong, their solstice stone alone would not be powerful enough to defeat Silas with the power of the other five stones at his call.

The day had come for Silas to put his plans into action, for many summers he had known what was needed for his journey to the underworld.

Even he, with his bountiful garden and magical store could not simply pick what was required from his garden. To enter the Underworld he would need a key and even then, the key would only work if his mind was able to travel the path. It was said that many had tried to enter the Underworld but had lost their minds along the way, the thought of this made Silas grin, and it wasn't a pleasant grin to behold, his face had begun to change as his thoughts had grown darker over the years. His once pale complexion, that had once made him appear youthful and handsome was now sallow, his green eyes had become such a dark shade of green they appeared almost black and the potions he had been drinking to strengthen his mind had begun to rot his teeth. He was no longer a picture of health and vitality as was usual for the Darach Nua but instead appeared gaunt and much older than his years and, it had to be said, quite deathly.

The deterioration of his appearance did not trouble Silas, for he was thinking about the long game, and he was fully aware that with each stone there was an eternal gift. Whoever was the keeper of the stone received that gift, once he had them in his grasp, his youth, strength and power would be eternal. So many scripts and scrolls he had read had told him of the possibilities, they told stories of the Underworld and those that had ventured there before him; their successes whilst short lived and their many failures. Silas had taken heed to all these tales and prepared for every eventuality, for where others had failed and returned with terrifying tales he had studied their failures, created potions of protection and trained his mind to prevent the Underworld from breaking him down. For Silas, the failures of others were his lessons in success.

Silas had known the day had come when the blossom had appeared on his apple tree; he had been watching and waiting. There had been an abundance of blossom earlier in the year, but as was always the way, the blossom gave way to fruit. As the tree finished bearing fruit the leaves would fall, but the tree was in full fruit, at its height of the harvest, the leaves would not begin to fall for another few weeks. None the less, there it was, apple blossom, as beautiful and delicate as it had been in spring. This was the key, his key to the Underworld, he must make a potion from the fruit, the blossom and the leaves that were all formed on the same branch and then create a staff from that branch.

He had read in the old writings and tales of other Underworld travellers of such a branch, but until he saw it with his own eyes he had been unsure if he would be able to cultivate it. The fact that it was there now, in front of his eyes, convinced him that this was his destiny, if it was not meant to be, the branch would not have grown he told himself.

Silas set about preparing the ceremony required for his journey. He could not call on the guardians to assist with his ceremony as his mother did, but he would need to invoke the elements to bring their power into his circle before his journey. He was concerned this would alert the guardians to what he was undertaking and because of this he had taken precautions, extra measures that he hoped would veil his circle long enough for him to complete his task. He did not want to stay long in the Underworld and if he worked quickly, he may go undetected.

The first step was his potion, he went into his cave and returned carrying a large athame. This was a long bladed magical knife with a black poplar handle, and it had a serrated edge, in fact it looked more like a small saw than a knife. Silas had made his athame the previous summer, he had created two handles, one he used for the athame and one was for the staff if and when the branch grew. He had spent a little time each day since their completion, polishing the black poplar handles and carving his name into them in traditional Darach Nua runes. He did this to ensure that each day as he polished and worked the handles he charged them with his energy, storing it up for his journey.

He took his athame to the apple tree and knelt on the ground before it, kissed his blade and leaned forward to kiss the bark on the trunk of the tree. As he did he thanked the tree for the gift he was receiving.

Reaching up he very carefully started to cut the branch; he could have cut through it quite quickly had he chosen to but he was afraid he would dislodge the fruit or the blossom or the leaves. Very slowly and carefully, it took Silas three hours to cut through the branch. As he made the last cut he carefully supported the weight to protect the fruit and the blossom. He was sweating heavily as he did this, not because the work had been particularly hard, the branch was no more than three inches in diameter, but because of the enormity of what the branch with its harvest represented to him and how long he had waited. Silas carefully carried the branch into his cave, for the remainder of his preparations he would need to work within his circle so he would need to ensure all that he needed to complete the process and go on his journey were contained within it.

With all his supplies and equipment to hand Silas began setting his circle, as he worked he thought of the many times as a child he had helped his mother with this, each time she called the guardians of the Quarters to watch over them during their circle work and provide the four elemental powers to their spell work. Silas grunted and shook his head at the thought, he could not call the Guardians but he still needed their powers. He had made a salt blend using dried salt crystals he had gathered over the last few years from the dankest darkest parts of the salt marsh. This was where the water was full of decay and empty of life, Silas hoped that by bringing the darkness of the Underworld into his circle of protection, the guardians would not feel the circle light.

He sprinkled the salt circle as wide as he could within his cave, despite it being called a circle, the shape he marked out in salt was anything but round, it was almost peanut shape if the truth was told. He walked the circle checking the edges to ensure there were no gaps, each step he also stopped to place a piece of mandrake root within the line of salt. He added the mandrake so that anyone, particularly the Guardians, who tried to see into his circle, would suffer from the anaesthetic symptoms of the Mandrake and be unable to interfere.

He walked the circle three times muttering as he went, "Round and round the circle's cast, joining present future, past."

With his circle defined, he would need to call the elements, this would be the test to see if he could go against the guardians using their own elements without their permission and remain undetected.

"Guardian of the Eastern tower, guard this circle with your power. Power of Air I call this night, protect this circle with all your might. Until I release you the circle you keep, between the worlds I intend to leap."

Silas called the element of Air and hoped the Guardian Ost would not be alerted; he took the branch from the apple tree and stuck it into the ground at the most eastern point of his circle to represent the element itself. He continued with his ceremony and called the elemental power of the South all the while hoping that Suth would not hear.

"Guardian of the Southern tower, guard this circle with your power. Power of fire I call this night, protect this circle with all your might. Until I release you the circle keep, between the worlds I intend to leap."

With the element of fire called, Silas took his athame to represent the element and stuck it into the ground in the most southern point of his circle.

Wind whistled through the cave and Silas stopped dead in his tracks, *was that Ost? he thought to himself, had he alerted them to his workings. He got a shiver down the back of his neck and all his hairs stood on end in anticipation of the confrontation. He listened, the wind whistled again and the trees rustled but nothing more. He shook his head, annoyed at the fact that he had so little confidence in his own ability. He had put up a veil that would last at least until he removed his circle, but he must work fast he did not know how long he would be in the Underworld.*

"Guardian of the Western tower, guard this circle with all your power.

Power of Water I call this night, protect this circle with all your might. Until I release you the circle keep, between the worlds I intend to leap."

Silas took a goblet filled with the dirty, dank water collected at the marsh and placed it at the most western point of his circle. Looking over his shoulder as he did, he was feeling uneasy, he needed to have all the quarters in place before his veil would work fully. Until then any one of the four guardians could detect what he was doing, and if any of them would, it be Siar, he knew Silas the best and would have been his guardian Silas thought, had his mother not interfered, forcing him he felt to leave and to follow his own path.

"Guardian of the Northern tower, guard this circle with your power. Power of Earth I call this night, protect this circle with all your might.

Until I release you the circle keep, between the worlds I intend to leap."

Silas reached into his pocket and took out an amber amulet, his mother had given this to him on the night he received his powers, a beautiful watery looking yellow and orange piece of amber set in a pewter mount, she had given it to him on the night of his ceremony. An amber pendant. To Silas this meant that she had known all along what his gift would be as Darach Nua, why else would she have given him a piece of amber, representing the element of Earth.

It was Siar who had spoken to him in the time leading up to his ceremony, so why was he given the gift of Herbal Law? Siar was the Guardian of the West, the element of water. Silas was convinced his mother had something to do with the gift he received as Darach Nua. That she had somehow limited the gift he received, was the only explanation for her giving him the amber. His resentment had started that day, when he had questioned her she had said that he was so knowledgeable with the plants and herbs that she had wanted him to follow in her footsteps as Hedge witch, but Silas did not believe her. He was sure she was trying to prevent him gaining power.

As he stared at the amber amulet in his hand, he again shook his head and grunted, he could not let images from his past slow him down now. He placed the amber to represent earth at the most northern point of his circle, as he placed the amulet into position the vibrations in the air changed, the sound of silence had changed to that of a low hum. Silas sat back on his heels and smiled, his circle was complete and the elements were guarding it. He closed his eyes and he could see in his mind's eye the blue energy circling, humming, pulsing and vibrating in perfect protection.

Silas had no time to sit back and enjoy the fruits of his labour yet, there was much work to do. He took an athame from his pocket, this one was much smaller, the blade only three inches long and the handle was made from bone and reserved only for magical work.

He walked over to the apple branch that was now standing like a single stem tree at the eastern point of his circle. He took his white bone handled athame and removed the apple, some blossom and three leaves, thanking the branch as he did. He carried them carefully to his cauldron that was bubbling away at the centre of the circle. As he sliced the apple and sprinkled the blossom and the leaves into his boiling pot he recited these words:

"Apple blossom, delicate and pink, give me clarity when I need to think. Apple fruit, so round and red, protect me in the land of the dead,

"Apple leaves, in shades of green, help me to remain unseen. Apple branch, my staff be true, guide my way in all I do."

The pot boiled furiously as the ingredients were added. Silas didn't stop but continued on with his preparations. He lifted the branch from the ground in the eastern side of his circle and used his athame to cut the branch in half, he replanted the smaller thin end of the branch into the ground carefully to ensure he didn't break the link with the elemental powers.

The thicker end of the branch he now took to the centre of the circle, he sat crossed leg and began to whittle his staff. He worked with precision and skill, gained from years of practice, within forty-five minutes he had the staff stripped back to reveal the beautiful bare applewood, free from bark, he added the handle of black poplar that he had been working on for so long then he reached further into his pocket and pulled out a long golden ribbon. Next he dipped the ribbon into the boiling pot until it was saturated with his potion and then took the steaming ribbon and began to wrapping it around the joint between the handle and the staff. As he tied the ribbon into place his hands were burnt from the heat of the boiling hot potion. He took some comfrey leaves and rubbed his hands together, dabbing the heat from them with the cold leaves, then threw the leaves into the pot. He held his staff up to admire its beauty and it was truly beautiful. It was time.

Silas gathered up the many pouches he had prepared and tied them to the string belt around his waist. He stopped for a moment as he realised he was smiling to himself, he laughed out loud as he knew his plans were playing out, just as he had planned, then he continued to gather his supplies. Mini vials of liquids and his many bags of herbs in place, he pocketed some precious stones to pay his way on the other side and then walked to his now still cauldron, with a ladle he carefully poured a generous helping into a bowl and as he waited for it to cool he prepared his bed.

A simple bed of straw was all that was required, Silas lay in the bed of straw thinking for a moment on what he was about to do. If there had ever been a moment when he questioned his own destiny it was right now. His mother's words raced through his head, images of past memories passed before his eyes. He closed his eyes and shook his head, he had come this far nothing was about to stop him. He lifted the bowl and drank the potion, clasped his new staff in both hands and lay back, waiting for the potion to start to work. He wasn't sure how long it would take but he knew he would be in a trance like sleep that he would hopefully wake from when his journey ended, this was the time, this is when Silas would leave being the lowly Darach Nua and gain the powers he had known he was destined to receive. As his thoughts wandered, his eyes started to droop, his eyelids were heavy and he could feel himself drifting into the Underworld.

Chapter Twelve
The Underworld

Silas could hear barking, his head felt fuzzy and he was confused. There it was again, was it a dog barking, no, it was dogs barking.

He rubbed his eyes and tried to sit up; as he did, he caught his staff in his cape and fell to the ground. Silas looked around and to his dismay he was still within the circle he had cast what felt like only moments before, was it moments? He felt as though he had only just closed his eyes but the light was somehow strange.

He sat up, staff still in hand and looked around, and something was different. He listened carefully, the dog barking had stopped, no, there it was again. He looked around but he couldn't see any dogs but something was different. The dogs stopped barking and it was silent. That was the difference. Where was the hum, the vibration? Was the circle broken? Silas jumped to his feet in sheer panic, if the circle was down the veil had gone and the guardians would detect what he was up to. Silas rushed over to his athame; if he could rework the circle, he may be able to replace the veil before he was detected. How had he failed?

What had he done wrong? These questions raced through his mind. He had researched his journey for so long that he couldn't believe it had ended before it had begun. As Silas reached for his athame his hand passed through it as though it was made of air. He stood bolt upright in surprise, what was going on? There it was again, dogs barking, and they were getting closer.

Silas spun around on his heels and looked around his cave, it was difficult to see, as it was so dark, his eyes darted to the fire in the centre of the circle, cold grey ashes were the only thing below his cauldron.

His mind was racing with all his thoughts, he felt dizzy. How long had he been in his trance the fire was blazing when he lay down only moments earlier.

There it was again, dogs barking.

Silas was getting angry now, more from frustration than anger itself. His trance work had failed, he had used the only leaf, blossom and fruit branch he had ever seen and now he had slept for who knew how long and the incessant dog barking was driving him insane, it was definitely getting louder.

Silas cried aloud in anger clasping his hands to his ears. He stopped, took a few deep breaths to compose himself and reached again for his athame. No, his hand passed through it as though he were a shadow.

His eyes scoured the circle, where was his staff? There it was in his humble bed of straw. He quickly retrieved it, this at least he could pick up, he marched towards the entrance to his cave, before he could think clearly, he would have to shut the dogs up.

Silas marched purposefully towards the entrance but it was not to be, as he attempted to step over the line of salt the circle walls reverberated and rebounded him back into the circle as though they were made of elastic. As Silas lay on his back in the middle of his cold dark circle, staff in hand, the barking stopped.

He sat up to listen. The sound he heard made the hairs on the back of his neck stand up and the spit in his mouth disappear. He tried to swallow to wet his mouth but it was no good, as he sat there shivering in fear he listened to the deep throat curdling growl of the dogs, they must be very close to his cave now. Silas scrambled to his feet and backed away towards the far side of his circle.

What was going on? What mistake had he made with his concoction? Had he lost his mind? Was he dead?

Silas waited; holding his breath and expecting a pack of dogs to come charging into the cave at any moment and tear him to pieces. As the dogs drew closer, Silas's thoughts turned to his mother, he shook his head. Why was he thinking of her at this moment? They had been so close once but now, he only held contempt for her, but in this moment, terrified and confused, the thought of his mother comforted him.

The sound was so close now. Silas gripped his staff with both hands, knuckles white from the sheer strength of his grip, waiting. He could hear their breath, panting and the sound of steps coming closer.

Silas stood perfectly still, frozen to the spot, but as he looked on he could not believe his eyes. The dogs or dog as it actually was, slowly walked into his cave, heads lowered and lips curled back as that deep curdling growl continued. The dog was the size of a Great Dane, dark charcoal grey in colour with three huge heads, each one rising from the thick neck of the muscle bound hound. Each head appeared to be independent as they growled, never for a moment taking their eyes off Silas. The hound walked around the circle perimeter. Silas could feel his body shaking uncontrollably and he tried to compose himself. The hound walked around Silas's circle, growling and watching him, drool dripping from its mouths. He could smell the hound; dirty, damp dog filled the air. It stopped in its tracks and turned its heads towards the cave entrance. Silas could hear footsteps approaching; he could hear the stones crunching on the ground.

Were there more to come?

The hound cowered down, whimpered, lowered its heads and darted towards the door wagging its three tails. Silas squinted to check he wasn't losing his mind; he wasn't, the hound's tails were snakes, three snakes with three heads hissing.

What had he done? Was he hallucinating?

The footsteps grew louder still and as Silas stared at the entrance to his cave a figure appeared in the doorway. Not at all what he had expected in his now overactive mind, there stood a small boy, the boy called to the hound to heel and it did instantly, lying quietly, panting at his feet.

"I see you have met Cerberus," the boy said in a calm quiet voice.

Silas struggled to speak, his mouth was now completely dry and his lips had stuck together. He coughed to clear his throat. "Cerberus" Silas croaked. He had read about Cerberus in his studies, but nowhere did it say he had three heads!

"Why have you come here?" asked the boy.

Silas cleared his throat again. "I came in the quest for help."

"And why would we help you? What can you offer us? Look at you, you are weak and afraid, there is nothing for you here."

The boy turned to leave but as he did, Silas called after him. "No, please, wait, I have something to trade, I am Darach Nua."

Silas ran towards the boy but again the circle deflected him, throwing him back to the ground, he was trapped within his own circle.

The boy stopped and appeared interested in what Silas had said. "The Darach Nua?" the boy asked, "How weak you have become. Cerberus, stay, guard the gates." The boy walked away shaking his head.

"Come back, please, don't leave me here, I'm trapped," Silas called after the boy, but the boy didn't even turn around to acknowledge Silas's words. Silas ran again at the circle and again it deflected him throwing back into the centre. Silas got up angrily he threw his staff at his cauldron but it passed straight through it as though it too were nothing more than a shadow.

For many hours, Silas paced up and down the length of his circular peanut shaped prison, trying to think of what had happened. He must have made it to the Underworld as many tales told of Cerberus guarding the gates, but he hadn't made it to the gates, he was still within his own circle in his cave. He looked over at the hound that was now sleeping; one head in the middle, each of the others lay to the side resting on one of his giant paws. He could still smell it, how could the smell penetrate his circle if he was trapped within, could the hound enter his circle? Silas shuddered at the thought.

His mind was now thinking more logically, if smell could enter the circle maybe it was only solid objects that could not. How would that help him he thought he was solid!

He checked his belt and touched the vials he had tied to it, was it the night before or only an hour before? He had lost all concept of time; at least he could touch the vials. Silas walked over to his cauldron and tried to pick up his flint to light the fire, no, his hand passed through it.

He reached to a bag on his belt and withdrew a pinch of herbs and powders, throwing them at the ashes of his fire he mumbled his words, trying to speak quietly so the hound would not be disturbed. The herbs instantly ignited. In the moment the flames appeared Silas remembered a time long ago when he had used the same combination and burned his sister's dress in the forest. For a moment he wished she were here with him. He stepped closer to the flames to warm his hands. There was no heat, he put his hand into the flames and there was nothing, he could see them but he could not feel them.

At least they gave light.

Silas lay on his straw bed, but in reality, he may as well have lay down on the bare floor as there was no comfort from the hay as he could not touch it or feel it. He put his head into his hands and sighed deeply he felt as though he were losing his mind, unable to determine what was real. He lay down, closed his eyes, and tried to sleep.

Sleep evaded him, his mind was far too active, and he thought over his journey so far, he laughed aloud at this journey? Where ever he had gone it wasn't far he was still in his own cave, worse again, he was still confined within his circle. He had made such preparations, expecting to go on such a long journey into the Underworld to find the help he sought, now he just wanted to wake up from this nightmare.

Cerberus lifted his heads; Silas heard it too, footsteps approaching. Silas got to his feet and waited, he tried to swallow but again his mouth was drying up; right now Silas did not care about the solstice stones or gaining power he just wanted to go home.

The boy appeared in the entrance to the cave, stroked the three heads of Cerberus and walked into the circle. He walked around Silas looking him up and down as he did.

"Sit, you can tell me why you think we would help you and what it is you think you can offer in return," the boy pointed to the ground beside the fire.

"Who are 'we'? "asked Silas, "Is it you that can help me?"

"No questions," said the boy.

Silas sat beside the boy and began to tell him all about his brother and sister and how together they were Darach Nua, how his siblings wasted their gift and how his mother allowed the guardians to rule her. He explained that he had tried to get to the Underworld because he needed the power from the stones to strengthen his magic and allow him to take the first five stones undetected and then finally the last stone from right under their noses.

The more he talked, the more he relaxed and he went into detail about his plans for taking control and being the only Darach Nua.

The whole time the boy sat and listened. Silas talked for what felt like hours and when he had finished he looked at the boy; the boy stood up and walked out of the circle,

"Wait, have you nothing to say? Can you help me?" Silas called after him.

The boy walked from the cave without turning his head, Cerberus plodding loyally behind him.

Silas sat alone in the centre of his circle beside the cold fire; he could do nothing to improve his situation. He thought of every possibility but each time he drew a blank. He could not tunnel from the circle as once the circle was cast it was not merely a dome over the consecrated ground but an actual full circular globe of protection that penetrated the earth below, or above? He thought if he was actually in the Underworld. He could not eat or drink, as he was unable to touch any object that had not been on his person when he started the journey. He couldn't even take down the circle as then the guardians would know where he was and that, he thought, would definitely be a fate worse than a cold circular prison.

He was at the mercy of the Underworld, in fact it appeared currently, that he was at the mercy of a small boy. He now understood why so many tales told of the travellers to the Underworlds losing their minds, he must stay strong and keep his mind active. If he ever came back here, not that this was something he currently desired, but if he did, he would make sure he had everything he needed on him rather than around him, that was a definite.

He looked over to the other side of his cave and he could see a basket of fruit, how good that would taste right now. His stomach must have recognised his thought as it started to grumble in protest at the lack of sustenance.

A thought popped into Silas's head as his stomach grumbled and he reached inside his cloak and removed a bag of rowan berries. As he poured them into the palm of his hand his thoughts again turned to his sister Rowan, so sweet, but so weak. He had brought the berries with him to help keep his mind clear which is definitely what he needed right now and also they were a great nutrient rich berry that may sustain him for a while. He sat there in the cold, nibbling on his berries feeling like he was having a veritable feast.

As Silas nibbled away an aroma started to fill the cave, he turned his head and sniffed as an animal would in the direction of the smell. He could smell pork, roast pork.

He stood up and walked towards the edge of the circle, not that he was going to attempt to pass through it again. He truly could smell a feast, the kind his mother would make for a celebration, with a pig on the spit roast and vegetables roasting in the fire. He closed his eyes and took a deep breath in through his nose to enjoy the smell, but now the smell was accompanied by sound, a low chattering sound. He could hear people, many people talking in the distance. Silas strained his senses to get as close to the source as he could. He closed his eyes and for a moment, he was in the forest at home, at his own ceremony about to receive his gifts, surrounded by the forest folk happily chattering away and feasting on the spit roast.

"Silas."

Silas opened his eyes and the boy was standing in front of him.

"Silas, it's time." The boy turned around and started to leave the cave, he looked behind to Silas and signalled for him to follow.

Silas had landed on his back in the centre of the circle once too often already. He poked the circle with his staff and this time it passed through, he followed the boy gingerly to the entrance of the cave. As they left the cave behind them Silas could not believe his eyes.

A huge pair of black gates stood just beyond his garden and he could see a large table through the gates set with a feast fit for a king. There were many people sat at the table enjoying the food and chattering away as though this were indeed a celebration.

As they walked towards the gates Silas looked around at his garden, the herbs and flowers were all withered and dead, all except the apple tree; each branch had a blossom, a leaf and a fruit on it and it was flourishing.

Cerberus was now lay across the gateway on guard. As the boy approached he plodded over to him, all three heads licking the boy's hands and his three tails hissing as they wagged. The boy took a large iron key from a belt around his waist and unlocked the gates. He opened the gate and signalled for Silas to walk through; as he did, the boy locked the gates behind them.

"Silas, come sit at the table I want you to meet my sister." The boy pointed to a chair for Silas to sit on.

Silas did as he was told and sat in a large high back dining chair. The boy's sister sat to his left at the head of the table, an empty seat beside him for her brother, the three of them were seated at the head of the huge table. The table itself looked as though it were made from a single fallen tree, a huge oak tree at that, as there were fifty or more 'guests' at the table. Carved into the table was the face of the Oak King, but it was not the face of the Oak King as Silas knew him, it was painful to see. In fact if it were not for the oak leaf crown, Silas did not think he would have recognised him. In Silas's own time the Oak King was a strong powerful God that he and his people worshipped, they would thank him at celebrations and harvest time, as he was the God of hunting and strength. The Lord of the Sun.

Silas ran his fingers over one of the carvings, the boy saw this. "There is no sun here, he is no God to us," spoke the boy.

Silas quickly removed his hand and placed it in his pocket.

The girl sitting to Silas's left tapped her spoon on her goblet; she stood up to address the feast. Silence instantly spread throughout the length of the table and all eyes were on her.

"We have an honoured guest seated at our table this night, Silas of the Darach Nua has come to us for help. We all knew this day would come and what must be done, I ask you all to raise your glasses and toast our guest, toast him by name."

With that, all the seated guests stood up and raised their glasses. "Silas of the Darach Nua." Their toast reverberated around the table, the sound made Silas feel weak and light headed.

"Be seated, you are weak and you need to feast." The girl pushed a plate to Silas.

"I'm sorry," replied Silas. "You are very generous to entertain me at your table and agree to talk with me, how rude of me, I do not know your names." Before Silas had barely the time to finish his sentence, silence befell the table again.

"And nor will you, to give someone your name is to give them power over you in this world and the next, we would not be so foolish as to arm you against us," the girl answered to Silas and with that the girl again raised her glass. The guests again stood and each of the fifty or more repeated her words.

"Silas, of the Darach Nua."

Silas looked up and down the length of the table, all the guests' goblets in hand, smiling, chanting his name, they all now had some kind of hold over him, he had not been as prepared as he thought.

This time the boy spoke. "You want the solstice stones and so do we, you want their power to rule the Darach Nua alone, we want their energy to charge the Black Sea, if you can cross the Black Sea we will help you, if you fail, the Darach Nua will be only two, do you accept the offer?"

Silas was trying to absorb what the boy had said, he had never heard of the Black Sea and swimming was not his greatest sport.

"We will need an answer this night, Silas of the Darach Nua," the girl added.

"Can I at least ask a few questions before I accept?" asked Silas meekly.

"You can ask three questions and then an answer will be required. If you accept the arrangement, we can discuss the possibilities of your success. If you do not accept, you must leave."

The girl sat down, picked up a large piece of pork, and began to eat. "Eat, Silas of the Darach Nua, you need your strength."

Silas picked up a piece of meat, juicy and pink with roasted crackling and started to eat; he was eating slowly trying to think of the best three questions he could. He knew he had already been outsmarted as each and every guest at the table knew his name, but this was why he had come, this was the purpose for everything. If he did not accept the challenge, it was all for nothing.

"Do I have to swim across the sea or can I build a raft?" asked Silas.

"That is two questions, what a foolish man you are," retorted the girl.

"No wait, I-I-I will change my question," stuttered Silas.

"You cannot change your questions when asked, you do not have to swim across the sea for it is as deep or as shallow as your mind, if you choose to make a raft then that is your choice. You have one question left."

This angered Silas and he squeezed the handle of his staff under the table to try to retain his composure. He must think, he must not waste his final question.

"On completion of my task will the powers you bestow on me be stronger than those forces I wish to rule, the Darach Nua, my mother, the guardians?"

If he could not outsmart his hosts, he could at least find out if the journey would be worth it. "It seems you are beginning to understand our ways," smiled the girl. "Yes, if you complete the task, you will take the power of the Underworld with you. Each stone you obtain you will become stronger as you will reverse the energy so that the sun no longer charges the stones, but the stones reflect all their energy into the Underworld, charging the Black Sea.

"If you succeed and obtain all six of the stones, you will be free of our bargain and retain your powers, until that day, we have a hold over you, Silas of the Darach Nua, and your powers can be removed by anyone sitting at this table."

The girl again raised her glass. "Silas of the Darach Nua."

The guests at the table all stood repeating her words.

"Then I accept your challenge." Silas raised his own glass and drank thirstily from it. The guests at the table all cheered at Silas's acceptance.

Chapter Thirteen
The Black Sea

For hours they talked of the journey ahead. Silas's new friends would not give him any information about the Black Sea or what would be required of him to cross it, or indeed for that matter, what would be on the other side, should he succeed.

They did however tell him of the potential for the power that he would possess if he were successful. The talk of this power that would grow with each stone acquired, excited Silas more than he expected. His mind had already moved forward in time to the point that he took his mother's stone, the final day, the final battle, if all that stood in his was the Black sea, he was ready.

The boy and the girl explained to Silas that he could take anything with him that he had prepared in his cave. This delighted Silas as he had made preparations for a long journey and had been so disappointed when he could not utilise his well-prepared supplies. He could take only what he could carry and no more.

The girl removed an amulet from around her neck, it was a black smooth stone on a black cord. She placed it around Silas's neck and as she did she spoke to Silas. "This stone is from the heart of the Black Sea, as the sea is charged by the solstice stones, this amulet will gain in power, as long as it is around your neck you will receive the power of the Black Sea and your powers will also grow with each stone collected."

Silas tucked the amulet inside his clothes, the stone was cold against his skin and he pressed it against his chest to warm it.

The girl continued. "Your staff is made from the branch of the apple tree that is the key to the gateway to our world, as long as you have this in your world, you will only need to touch your staff to the ground to use your powers, but guard it well, the powers are limited. If you lose the staff, you will lose the powers."

Silas stroked the handle of his staff, he knew when he had made it that it would be important to get him to the Underworld, he had no idea it would be a key to his powers.

The boy and the girl walked with Silas, opening the gateway on the way to the cave. Once inside the cave, Silas quickly set about gathering his tools and supplies for his journey. It was difficult to pack as he had no idea how far his journey would take him, or how long it would take to complete. His bags packed, he stopped and looked around the cave, knowing that this may be the last time he saw it either in this world or his own.

The boy and girl walked with Silas back through the gateway, passing Cerberus, who seemed to be fast asleep, his three heads relaxed and lay across his paws, but as he slept his tails continued to hiss.

The girl stopped to lock the gateway, as she did, Silas turned to look at the guests at the feast. He was shocked to see the table was now empty of guests. The food remnants were rotten and the glasses empty, cobwebs adorned the chairs where he had sat only an hour earlier, he turned to his hosts. "How long have I been in the Underworld?"

"Our time is not like your own, Silas of the Darach Nua, we have no sun to measure the days, you can grow old in a moment if you do not use your time well, but each time the Black Sea is charged you will regain some of your lost youth."

Silas heard the words the girl spoke but he did not understand, yes, with no sun it would be difficult to measure night and day, but he had been here, well, he didn't actually know, maybe a day or two, maybe three? As he stepped forward, he used his staff as a walking stick and saw his own hand, the skin now wrinkled and blotched with age spots. He touched his hair, it felt longer, thinner and coarse.

"You need to cross the Black Sea before your time here ends your time everywhere, you are a mortal in an immortal world."

Silas turned to look at the girl, fear in his eyes and his heart pounding but she was nowhere to be seen, he stood alone on a dirt track. He could see a large expanse of water ahead, how far away was that? He squinted to take in the full view in the distance, he could only guess, maybe a mile, or two?

As Silas walked alone on the dirt track heading towards the sea in the distance, his bags were getting heavier and his steps slower.

It began to rain and the wind blew through his clothes, chilling his bones. He walked for what seemed like hours but the sea ahead was no closer. He couldn't help but wonder to himself, was this another trick of the Underworld? Would he ever reach the Black Sea or would he die, old and cold in the Underworld?

Silas turned a corner on the winding dirt road and to his surprise he saw a light flickering in a cave. He stopped and rubbed his eyes; this was the first sign of life he had seen. He picked up his pace at the thought of human contact and warmth. A moment's escape from the driving rain and wind may help him to clear his mind.

Silas slowed as he approached the entrance to the cave, he could see flames flickering on the wall from a fire within. He walked into the mouth of the cave, took a deep breath and stood as straight as his now ageing body would allow.

"Welcome, Silas of the Darach Nua." The voice came from the back of the cave and he could not see who the voice belonged to, did everyone in this world know his name? "Sit beside the fire and dry your clothes, your journey has barely begun and you appear as though you are almost at your end."

Silas did as he was instructed and sat beside the fire. This time, he could at least feel the warmth, as he sat there shivering, feeling completely sorry for himself and out of his depth, a young woman emerged from the darkness at the back of the cave.

"Drink this tea, it will rejuvenate you, do not think I am your friend or your servant, but I know the quest you are on. If you succeed we will all benefit from the trade."

Silas looked at the young woman, she was very beautiful with long raven black hair and an ivory white complexion. She passed him a bowl of steaming tea.

"Before I drink this, tell me what it is, my apologies kind friend, but I can trust no one in this place." Silas's body was ageing quickly but his mind was as active as ever.

The young woman laughed. "It is a tea made from the flowers of immortelle, nothing more than flowers and leaves, but drink it now and it will reverse at least some of your ageing, you may then at least stand a little chance of success."

Silas raised the bowl to his face, to his horror he could see his own reflection in the liquid in the bowl. His own once black hair was white and wispy, soaked against his now wrinkled and aged face. What had he done coming to this place? He raised the bowl to his mouth and drank it down, gulping like an animal that had been in the hot sun with no shade. The drink warmed him initially on the inside but as he calmed and warmed by the fire, he felt strange. He could feel the blood pumping through his veins, not the feeling of his heartbeat as in times of fear but his blood travelling through his veins. He looked down at his hands and the age spots were fading before his eyes. He stretched and yawned and his back felt stronger, he was able to fully stretch and sit up without aches.

He looked over to the young woman who was now sat plaiting her hair, the thinnest finest braid he had seen. When she was done she tied more hair to secure the braid at the top and the bottom and then took an athame from beside the fire and removed it.

"I suppose I cannot ask your name?" asked Silas, again regretting the moment he had given his in his cave.

"I have no name, I am the Seer," the woman replied. Silas was unsure if he had misheard her.

He looked up from the fire. Silas did not understand. "You are Siar?"

Again, the woman laughed at Silas, this time moving her dark locks back from her face. "No, I am not Siar. I am The Seer."

As Silas looked on, the woman came closer to the fire, now she had moved her hair back he could see her eyes were white, totally white, the woman who described herself as the Seer, could not see, she was blind.

"Oh, I am so sorry I didn't realise," apologised Silas. "I, I thought you had said Siar, Siar is a guardian from my own world, I didn't realise you were, well, err, without sight." Silas tried to recover as diplomatically as he could but he could feel the colour rising in his cheeks.

"Don't apologise, and there is no need to be embarrassed or blush, it is my choice to see what others do not. I am far from without sight."

"How did you know? How could you see?"

Silas didn't understand how she could know he was blushing. He stood up and stepped back from the fire, nothing was as it seemed in this place. Why had he come here?

The woman stepped forward and held out her hand, "Come sit with me and let me see for you, I may be able to help you on your way."

Silas was wary of accepting any further help, in fact he was wary of everything and longed for the simplistic life he had left behind, what price would this 'help' be?

"The charge will not be great," spoke the Seer. "How? You read my thoughts?"

The Seer stepped forward. "I told you I see what others do not, let me help you with my gift and in return I will gift you sight. Not like my own but enough to help, and should you succeed on your quest we will both benefit. Wear this."

The Seer held out the braid she had made from her own hair.

"As your powers grow, so will mine, it will take nothing from you but as long as you wear this token, I will gain strength from you. Wear it until you no longer have use of the sight or you are unable to use it and our link will then be broken and your debt paid."

Silas thought for a moment, he could wear it until he no longer wanted the sight and then his debt would be paid? That sounded reasonable, but he was untrusting of his new friend, but without her help he may not make it through his quest.

"Let me rest here for the night out of the rain and the wind. Let me recover some of my strength and my youth, you can see for me and if I think what you see is of help I will wear your token. If not I shall leave and we will owe each other nothing."

"Silas of the Darach Nua you are not as foolish as some may think. You learn our ways quickly, of this I am glad, for I will benefit as much as you from our trade. If we work together we will both prosper, I wish you no harm but no favours will I give. I am not your friend, if we understand this we will both gain only what we need and lose nothing."

Silas and the Seer sat around the fire and chatted for hours, he drank more of the immortelle tea and rested in a warm dry bed of animal skins. As he lay there his eyes beginning to droop from tiredness, his mind wandered over the last few days and of course, the days ahead. No wonder so many returned with their minds gone, this place was unhealthy, unearthly and far more dangerous than he had thought from the safety of his cave. Tomorrow was a new day, he would see what the Seer could tell him to help him on his quest, then, maybe, only maybe, they would make an alliance. With that thought in his mind Silas drifted off into a much needed sleep.

Silas was restless throughout the night, despite sleeping deeply, his mind wandered between the worlds, visions of his mother and the guardians towered over him whilst he slept. Images of the guests at the dining table interjecting with telling comments of his current journey, in the distance he could hear the Seer, he followed her voice and she led him to his own cave, just as he had left it, warm, dry and safe, in this place in his dreams, Silas slept soundly for the next few hours, surrounded by familiar smells and home comforts.

Silas woke to the sound of a crow, squawking, not just squawking, but squawking and walking on his chest. He opened his eyes and the crow looked at him, cocked his head to one side as though getting the measure of him, then flew away.

Silas sat up and looked around his surroundings. The fire was now only smoking embers but he could still feel some heat from it. As he moved closer out of instinct to feel its warmth, he heard a sound behind him. He turned around and saw the Seer entering the cave with her arms full of firewood. Silas jumped up to help her and took the wood from her and placed it beside the smoldering embers.

Silas began to place the wood on the fire, each piece carefully placed to build a tower, to allow the flames to climb. He heard his mother's voice as he did, she had taught him so many years before when lighting a fire at the home place. "Fire wants to climb, Silas, give it the framework and watch it climb."

His mother had taught him many things over the years, things he had forgotten until he had needed them.

"It is time Silas." The Seer touched his arm to get his attention and then walked over to a table towards the back of the cave, dimly lit with stubs of candles.

Silas looked at the fire, now jumping and climbing through his structure, he thought to himself, give it the framework and watch it climb. He took a deep breath and went over to the table and sat down.

"You are rested, you are more youthful than you were this last night and the time has come to see." The Seer held out her hands across the table to Silas as she spoke.

Silas was afraid, everything about this place scared him, would it ever be worth it? He inhaled deeply and as he slowly let out his breath, he held his hands out across the table to the Seer.

"The Black Sea is your quest," said the Seer. She squeezed his hands and continued to speak.

"The Black Sea is your quest, its reach is deep, but its bed is dry. You need to open the door to the other side, when the door has been opened, the balance will transfer. The waves will come and the thirst will be quenched. Be aware, the door once opened will reveal your true nature in this world and the next, this cannot be undone.

You cannot hide, when the door is opened, you are of our world, Silas of the Darach Nua, they that protect the stones will know you as their enemy, they will defend against you with all their powers in the past, the present and the future, time cannot heal that which cannot be undone.

Open the door and it can never be closed. This is your choice."

The Seer released Silas's hands and sat back on her stool. She looked directly at Silas, white eyes appearing to see nothing but yet seeing deep into his soul.

Silas stood up and stepped back from the table, he didn't like how this made him feel, could he trust what she said?

"Fire wants to climb, Silas." He looked sharply at the Seer, as it was not her own voice she spoke with, but that of his mother's. "I see all that has been, all that is here and all that is yet to come." This time she spoke as the Seer, this at least was something, Silas found it very unnerving when he had heard his mother's voice from her lips.

"Will I succeed in my quest? Will I charge the Black sea? Will I see my world again to use my new powers in my quest against my enemies?"

Silas was almost stuttering he was so anxious to find out the answers to his questions. "Silas, I cannot give you the answers to all your questions, but I can tell you this, the Black Sea will be charged and your enemies will have a formidable opponent in future battles, if you win or lose these battles depends on how you use your new powers."

A grin grew across Silas's face, he replayed The Seer's words in his mind, "How he would use his new powers," this was enough for him to *decide to make the trade.*

"Give me your sight, let us trade." Silas held out his hand to seal the deal, as he did he saw the braided token was on his wrist. Had it been there all along?

Silas packed his belongings and prepared to set off on his quest. "How will I know I have your sight? Will it just appear to me?"

Silas looked to The Seer for a response, he could not help but be suspicious in this place, nothing was ever as it seemed and he did not want to walk away having agreed a deal, only to find out later he had been duped.

"When it is needed it will be there, the sight is your own and you will see it as you do your own thoughts or memories, no one can see it but you, if you remove the token our link is broken and the sight will leave you,"

"Thank you, I have a feeling we may meet again."

Silas walked out of the Seer's cave and down the dirt track. As he approached the bottom of a steep incline the trees started to close in; initially he was happy about this as it provided him with some shelter, but the further he found himself within the forest the more he felt uneasy. The trees were large old oak trees but they were so dense within the forest that little light made it through to the forest floor, he was feeling his way through in almost complete blackness. He stopped on a number of occasions, he was sure he heard someone or something following behind him.

Silas had been walking for hours, he was cold and exhausted. He stepped over a fallen tree and decided it was time to take a moment to rest. He placed his belongings on the floor beside the fallen tree and lit a small fire, it was little comfort in the dark, damp loneliness of the forest.

Leaning forward to find a comfortable place to sit on the fallen tree, he was taken over for the first time by the sight. He could see the very forest he was now in but it was much lighter, the trees were not so dense and he could hear footsteps approaching. He looked around he could not believe the sight before his eyes, it was boy of about thirteen-years-old, dressed in strange clothes running through the forest and he appeared to be chasing someone.

The boy shouted to someone ahead of him, "Who are we running from?" The voice that followed made Silas's blood run cold.

"From Silas, go quietly or he will hear you," the figure ahead replied to the boy.

Silas snatched his hand from the tree in fear, he knew that voice, it was Siar, the Guardian, what was he doing here in the forest in the Underworld? Was he even here? The Seer had said he could see all that was, all that is and all that would be. Who was the boy? Silas had never seen anyone dressed like that before.

Did Siar now know where he was? He couldn't take a chance. Silas gathered his belongings and began to run through the forest. As he approached a clearing, he could see a body of water ahead, it was now or never. Silas ran and dived into the water.

If this was the Black Sea, he needed to cross it now. He dived deep into the Black Sea but found that he could not get back to the surface, he kicked and kicked but the surface was nowhere in sight. He checked his bubbles as he had been taught as a child, sometimes underwater you lose your bearings and without realising it you are swimming deeper rather than to the surface. His brother Sean had taught him that, but no, the bubbles were rising. Silas kicked furiously for the surface, how deep into the water had he dived? He pushed harder and harder for the surface as he did he hit his head on something wooden, he felt around and above his head, was this how he was to die, struggling for breath trapped in a body of water, unable to find his way to the surface? He was panicking now as the last of the oxygen left his body. With his last ounce of strength, he pushed towards the wooden object that he had struck his head on and his hand clasped onto something metal and cold. He pulled the metal towards him and a door opened downwards. Silas scrambled to the edge of the opening taking huge deep breaths, each one filling his lungs, the same lungs that only a second earlier he had thought were about to collapse.

Silas pulled himself up and out of the freezing cold water and into the room above. Shivering, shaking and numb from the experience he looked around at his surroundings. He could see his reflection in a mirror on the opposite wall, he was shocked at how he had changed, his face looked aged and his once black hair now was adorned with a pure white fleck running down the side of his face. He looked at his hands, *they too had aged but the age spots had not returned so he had regained at least some of his youth.*

He stood up slowly, still shaken from the experience, but as he stood there beside the door in the floor, looking around the room he had entered, a chill ran down his spine, he froze to the spot and every hair on his body was standing on end. He had been here before, many times. Silas's mind was racing, was he back in his own world, he must be, he knew this place.

This was the Tower of Siar, the Guardian of the West.

Chapter Fourteen
Watching and waiting

"That doesn't tell us much," Elliott said sitting back on the bed. "We already knew that Silas was about to do something bad to the Darach Nua, we need to know what he did, and can we change it?"

"How can we change it?" Mark added. "Isabella said it was, what? Thirteen hundred years ago, it's not like we can go back in time, it's already happened."

"But," said Roisin, "if it's already happened to the Darach Nua, has it already happened to old Darach Nua or to us? And we don't know what we can do yet, we won't find out until the solstice. We need to read more, find out what Silas did, why has there been no Darach Nua for thirteen hundred years?"

"Darach Sean," Elliott added.

"What?" asked Roisin.

"You asked did it happen to old Darach Nua, or us. The old Darach Nua are called Darach Sean, remember, Isabella told us."

"Yes, she did, I had forgotten," said Roisin.

"Come on, Roisin, Elliott," said Mark. "Why have you stopped reading? We don't have time to chat, get reading."

The three cousins all lay back down on the bed in a line, heads propped up by their hands on their elbows.

"OK, I will carry on." Roisin opened the book at the page she had just closed. The page was blank.

"Not again!" shouted Elliott. "We don't have time for disappearing pages, it's Tuesday tomorrow. That means we only have twenty-four hours until the solstice, what use will our powers be if we don't know what we are supposed to do with them when we get them?" Elliott flopped back on the bed, clearly frustrated.

"What are we going to do?" asked Mark

Elliott sat up sharply. "Mark, look through the window, is there a light on at Isabella's?"

Mark dashed over to the window. "Yes! All her lights are on, the house is lit up like a beacon!"

The three cousins looked at each other. Roisin was first to speak. "Well you are all thinking it so I will say it, it's only nine p.m., Isabella is clearly still awake, shall we pay her a visit?"

"What will Nanny say?" said Elliott.

"I don't know about you, but I wasn't planning on asking her?" said Roisin.

"OK, but we need to at least leave a note, we could say we saw a gate open on the farm and went to close it," said Elliott. "Don't look at me like that, if she realises, we are gone she'll be worried and I don't want Nanny tramping through the fields in the dark looking for us, she might get hurt."

"Elliott has a point," said Mark. "Maybe we should just tell Nanny we going to check on Isabella because all the lights are on."

"I suppose we could just do that," said Roisin. "Sorry I think I'm getting carried away with the adventure and excitement, I feel like we are characters in a story this is all so unbelievable."

"Don't worry, Roisin, we will keep you grounded." laughed Mark. "Come on, let's find Nanny."

The three cousins got their coats and shoes on and headed down to the kitchen, when they got there to their surprise Nanny was sitting at the kitchen table with her coat and wellies on. "Have you been out, Nanny?" asked Elliott.

"Not yet," replied Nanny smiling. "Are we ready? We don't want to be out too late if we are walking across the fields. Mark, have you got your torch?"

"Err, yes, Nanny," Mark replied a little puzzled. "Where are we going?"

"So much time to cover and so little time to cover it in," said Nanny, "Old Isabella's of course, with any luck she will have a roaring fire going, you never know just what we might see."

The three cousins stared at each other in amazement, how could Nanny know? but then, how could she not know? and who else knew?

They followed Nanny out of the back door in silence in a perfect well-formed line. Just as Roisin was about to close the door Nanny turned around. "Wait, aren't you forgetting someone?"

Nanny gave one of her knowing smiles. Roisin opened the door wide and Gypsy and Benjy came bounding out together. Roisin was about to close the door and Nanny again stopped her. "Not quite yet," Nanny said. The three cousins looked at each other puzzled, then they heard the little yaps and Flossy came trotting out.

"Nanny! She is too small to come with us and auntie Jess won't like her getting muddy," protested Elliott.

"She won't get muddy if I carry her," Jess said as she followed Flossy through the back door smiling. "Let's go, we have a long night ahead of us and you didn't think I would let you go without me."

"Does anyone know what is going on?" Mark whispered to Roisin.

"Everyone, except us it seems," said Roisin.

With that the five of them set off across the field with Gypsy, Benjy and Flossy in tow. "Auntie Jess," said Mark, "have you always known, well known, who we were?"

"Not always, but as long as I have known who I am, I have known who you are," replied Jess.

"So, you're not Jess?" asked Mark.

"Of course I'm Jess, but I am also your Watcher."

"What is our Watcher?" Mark asked, more confused by this new information he had been given.

"I watch over you, even when I'm not with you I am watching, and if you need me, I will know."

"Sort of spying on us?" asked Mark. He wasn't sure he liked the idea of Auntie Jess always watching him.

Jess laughed. "No not like spying, I can't see you with my eyes I can feel your energy."

Mark much preferred this idea, he ran ahead to tell Roisin and Elliott of this new information. As the three of them walked ahead with Nanny and Jess following, they discussed their escorts. If Nanny and Auntie Jess knew they were Darach Nua, did their mothers know too? Did their fathers?

"Nope, just us," shouted Jess from behind them. Nanny and Jess thought this was very funny.

"And don't worry, Mark, I wasn't watching, you are just not very good at whispering."

As they walked towards Isabella's house, lights shone from every window. "She must have every light in the house on," commented Mark.

"She doesn't have any lights," replied Elliott. "There is no electricity up here remember, she must be burning a hundred candles!"

They made their way down the garden path and as Elliott was about to knock on the door it opened. "Come in, come in, come in," said Isabella, "What kept you all so long? We have much to discuss."

Elliott was right, there were candles burning on every window sill and every spare bit of space on every shelf and the kitchen looked beautiful. It was like stepping back in time, with Isabella's odd jars and bottles and herbs hanging from the ceiling. It would not have been out of place on the pages of a history book.

"Isabella?" asked Mark. "Are you afraid of the dark?"

Isabella looked sharply at Mark, put her hands on her hips and began to laugh. "Afraid of the dark?" Isabella was holding her ribs now she was laughing so hard. "No, my young friend, I am not afraid of the dark, the dark is afraid of me!" With that Nanny and Auntie Jess joined in the laughter.

"I'm sorry, Mark," said Isabella "We are not laughing at you, but at the thought of you thinking I was afraid of the dark. I lit the candles for the three of you, I thought you might be afraid of the dark walking up to Widdershins at night."

"You said Widdershins," spotted Elliott. "You have never referred to the farm as Widdershins before, it was Shin's Farm?"

"It's Shin's farm to the Dall, you are not the Dall any more my Darach Nua. You are not blind from the truth and I told you I will never tell a lie to the Darach Nua. This place has been Widdershins since long before the bricks around us stood here. Since this was the place that the sun stone rested in nothing more than a cave in the forest."

"The sun stone?" asked Elliott, is that Silas's mother's stone? Is it here?"

"Before I answer any more questions or we discuss the past, the present or the future, we must cast the circle; tonight you will see things you have only read about or heard in the whispers of your mind, but you are safe here. I will call the guardians to protect our circle and we will all be safe, then we can discuss what has been and what will be."

"The guardians?" Mark piped up. "Is Siar coming here tonight?"

"If I cast our circle well, Siar will be here tonight and he will not be alone, tonight is the first gathering of the forest folk in thirteen hundred years." With that Isabella disappeared into a room off the kitchen.

"Nanny?" Roisin looked to Nanny and her face said more than words could describe.

"My little squirrels, come to me, would I ever put any one of you in danger? You are my world and I will protect you with my life, I would not have brought you here for this if I did not think you were ready, I will be here with you at all times and so will Jess."

With that Nanny held out her arms and Roisin, Mark and Elliott ran into them. As Nanny held out her arms, Jess joined their little circle and Nanny and Jess wrapped their arms around them.

Isabella emerged from her room carrying a wide topped wicker basket. "Michelle, I need your help to cast the circle, I need you to know for the future in case anything happens to me." As Isabella spoke, she looked at Nanny.

The cousins looked at each other, it was strange to hear Nanny called by her Christian name, they knew her name was Michelle, but nobody used it, they called her Nanny and their parents called her Mammy. Roisin was baptised Roisin Michelle in honour of Nanny, but it was strange to hear. They huddled closer to Jess as Nanny helped Isabella with her preparations.

Isabella took an old twig broom from beside the fire and began to sweep the floor. "Jess, why is Isabella cleaning if we have so much to do?" asked Mark.

"She is not cleaning as we would think of it," replied Jess. "She is cleansing the space, in olden times the besom, that's the broom, was used to cleanse negativity from a space before the circle was cast. Isabella does things the old way, the right way."

Isabella replaced the broom beside the fire. "Are we ready?" Isabella looked at her guests who were all now silently staring, "Let's begin."

Roisin reached out on either side, taking Mark's hand in one hand and Jess's hand in the other. Jess responded squeezing Roisin's hand and taking Elliott's hand in the other.

Isabella began.

"Guardian of the Eastern tower, guard this circle with your power, Power of Air I call this night, protect this circle with all your might. Until I release you the circle keep, between the world's I intend to leap."

As Isabella spoke, she took a large conch shell from her basket and placed it at the eastern edge of her circle.

"Guardian of the Southern tower, guard this circle with your power, Power of fire I call this night, protect this circle with all your might. Until I release you the circle keep, between the worlds I intend to leap."

With the element of fire called, Isabella took an athame from her wicker basket to represent the element and stuck it into the ground in the most southern point of her circle.

"Guardian of the Western tower, guard this circle with all your power. Power of Water I call this night, protect this circle with all your might. Until I release you the circle keep, between the worlds I intend to leap."

Isabella took a goblet filled with the water and placed it at the most western point of her circle. "Guardian of the Northern tower, guard this circle with your power. Power of Earth I call this night, protect this circle with all your might. Until I release you the circle keep, between the worlds I intend to leap."

Isabella looked to Elliott. "Do you have your amulet?"

Elliott looked at his cousins, he hadn't mentioned the amulet part of his story to them. He reached inside his shirt and removed the amber amulet from around his neck, his face flushed as he did. Roisin and Mark looked at each other and then at Elliott, why had he kept this from them.

Isabella took the amulet from Elliott and placed it at the most Northern area of the circle, as she placed the amulet on the ground, wind rushed into the kitchen and the windows rattled. There was a change in the atmosphere of the room and you could hear a feint hum all around, it was the same hum the cousins heard earlier when Roisin placed her hand on the book.

There was a knock at the door, Isabella took her wand from her apron and drew an invisible square in the air.

"Nanny, what is she doing with that stick?" whispered Mark.

"It's not a stick, it's a wand, and she's making a doorway in the circle, once the circle is cast you can't just walk through the edges or you break the circle," explained Nanny.

"Why is she doing that?" whispered Mark again.

"Because someone has just knocked on the door, how else will Isabella leave the circle to answer it if she doesn't create a door in the circle," Nanny smiled at Mark as she explained.

"So, who's at the door?" Mark asked Nanny.

"Well, Mark, we won't know that until Isabella opens it will we," laughed Nanny.

Isabella opened the door and four extremely tall gentlemen walked in, they appeared the same yet somehow individual. The first one to enter the room, loomed tall above Isabella and he had to lower his head and stoop slightly to allow for the beams of the kitchen ceiling as he entered. He carried a white staff in one hand, his hand curled over the top of the staff, long thin fingers and old yellow nails. His skin was pale and grey and wrinkled with age. His eyebrows that were just visible under the hood of his cape were long and white and wispy. As he removed his hood and looked at his host, you saw his gentle green eyes, so soft they made his face warm and friendly despite the cold wrinkled appearance of his skin.

"My Lady Isabella," he said as he sat at one of the corner chairs of the kitchen table and smiled warmly at his host, a smile of friendship but also of worry.

"My Lord, you are welcome," Isabella waved her hand to the three remaining corner chairs to direct the three other gentlemen to their seats. They would have to be seated as the four of them filled the small kitchen towering over the other guests. Isabella turned to face her other guests. "Now the Guardians of the Quarters are here we may begin."

Roisin squeezed Nanny's hand, hard. "Nanny, is this really happening?"

Mark stepped beside Nanny and Roisin, "Roisin, that's Siar," Mark nodded his head towards the younger looking of the four gentlemen.

Their guest saw this and nodded in recognition. "Mo Chara," he said looking directly at Mark.

Mark nodded back in response but the colour had drained from

Mark's face. He turned to Roisin. "Tell me I am dreaming again, this can't be happening, I think I feel sick."

"Nanny," Roisin nudged Nanny to get her attention. "Isabella." Nanny spoke to Isabella as though they were old friends. "This is a lot for our young ones to take in, I think they should sit and take something sweet," Nanny put her arms around Mark's shoulders to bolster him.

Elliott was not in the least taken aback by this encounter, he stood tall in the middle of the room, beaming, "Isabella, let me help." He walked over to Isabella still grinning profusely and began to make tea.

"Elliott, I do believe you are enjoying yourself" Isabella said to Elliott smiling.

"Isabella, I just can't help it, I have this warm fuzzy feeling in my belly, it's better than Christmas Eve!"

Isabella laughed with Elliott at his honest confession. "Enjoy the feeling while you can, we have much work to do and I'm afraid it won't all be so pleasant, but, Elliott, I want you to know, I am so proud of you and I know you will do what is required."

Isabella put her arm around Elliott's shoulders and gave him a comforting squeeze. Elliott didn't need comfort, right at this moment he felt as tall as the guardians.

With the tea made and home-made biscuits to share, they now all sat around the huge table in the kitchen lit by half a dozen candles.

Isabella was the first to speak. "It has been thirteen hundred years since the last gathering around my hearth, we do not have a lot of time but I know, if we work together and only work for good, we can succeed with our challenge."

Tuath tapped his glass and looked to Isabella. "Lady Isabella, we have much to do as you and I know, but have you explained to our friends what is required before the ceremony?"

Isabella looked at Tuath and her face revealed more than she normally would allow. She seemed to wince at the thought of what Tuath had said. "Not yet, Tuath, but I will."

Isabella looked around the table, at Roisin, Mark and Elliott, then to Nanny and Jess. "You must believe me when I say this, you are all my descendants, if you were not, you would not be here around my table, you are here to help me close a chapter and start a new one."

Jess looked at Mark, he was still pale. "Marky, don't be afraid, I'm here with you," she squeezed his hand and he returned her a gentle meek smile. "Do you know how special you are to be sat here, this proves you are descended from great warriors of the past, just believe in yourself and you will be fine."

"Fine?" Mark thought, right now he was concentrating on not being sick and ruining the evening. Yes, he was excited, who wouldn't be, but he had a sick feeling in his stomach that he couldn't shake and his mouth was watering.

Isabella spoke again. "There can only be one Darach Nua. A long time ago, thirteen hundred years to be precise, a spell was cast that froze the Darach Nua's powers, transforming them so they could no longer use their powers for evil. You know Silas was of the Darach Nua and this was the only way to stop him, sadly, in order to stop one Darach Nua, we had to stop all three.

"Before you can receive your powers, we have to release the Darach Sean, that is the old Darach Nua, their powers need to be released before you can receive yours.

The Darach Sean are close by, as your ceremony grows closer they will feel the veil lifting and the tingle of the powers they once had. As you align in spirit with them you will feel their energy. Mark, this is why you feel sick, you are strong and have great potential but you are younger than your cousins. This will be difficult for you until you receive your powers as you are not yet thirteen. You are the first Darach Nua to ever receive their powers early, but you are a strong young man from a strong Celtic family. Whilst it will be harder for you, this would not be happening if you were not able for it.

"The Darach Sean know this and will try to connect with you. But remember, the Darach Sean are three, but only Silas is your enemy. We must try to protect Sean and Rowan, they did nothing wrong and have been trapped for thirteen hundred years due to Silas's actions."

Elliott coughed. "Ahem, when you say close, how close do you mean?"

"They have been here all along Elliott, but not in human form, not for thirteen hundred years."

Isabella looked so sad, Roisin touched her hand. "They are the horses aren't they?" Roisin spoke clearly and without fear.

"The three horses are the Darach Sean, and the black angry horse is Silas."

Roisin wasn't asking the question, she was confirming a fact, she knew it to be true, she didn't know how, she just knew.

"Yes, Roisin, the two bays and the black stallion in the top paddock are the Darach Sean."

"That's why they were acting so strange when we first met, the two bays were preventing the black stallion from approaching us near the fence," said Elliott. "Or should I say Sean and Rowan were keeping Silas from getting too close! Flippin eck! Silas has been here the whole time!"

"Won't Silas be angry when the spell is lifted?" asked Mark, looking paler by the minute.

Siar looked at Mark and replied. "He will, Mo Chara, but the spell or the veil, however you choose to describe it, won't be lifted until the moment you are to receive your powers. This is why for the first time in history, three Darach Nua will receive their powers simultaneously. You will all be gifted your powers at the same moment. We will all be there with you to protect you and when your ceremony is over, Silas will have no powers in this time, but we do not know all his secrets from his dealings with the Underworld, he may be able to go back"

"Back where?" asked Mark.

"Back to the time that the spell was cast, back in time to prevent our victory over him thirteen hundred years ago," Siar explained. He then took a vial from his pocket. "Mark, drink this, it will help ease the energy drain that you are feeling and you may not feel as sick. Just sip it as and when you need to and try to keep Silas from your mind, it is there that he is drawing strength from you."

Mark took the bottle and looked at Jess. "It's OK, Marky, Siar is our friend he wouldn't give you anything that would hurt you. I can take a sip too if you like."

Mark smiled meekly back at Jess and took a sip from the bottle.

Nanny spoke up. "I think Mark should rest, Silas feels his youth and is draining his energy. Mark can hear as well lying down as he can sat at the table."

"I'll go with him," said Jess and led Mark to lie on a deep window seat that was like a bench. She then covered him up with one of the patchwork blankets, knitted from many different colours and sewn together by hand. As soon as Jess covered him up, Mark was asleep.

"It's hitting him hard, very quickly," said Isabella. "We need to protect him until the solstice. On this night I will recount to you the story of thirteen hundred years ago when Silas had been to the Underworld, he had escaped through the Black Sea into Siar's tower. When he returned to this world, he used his new-found powers to take five of the solstice stones, one remained, the sun stone.

"The story I will tell you was of that last night, but listen well because we may have to revisit that time and that place together. If we do, we cannot make any mistakes, some of us have lived that night before and this includes Silas, he will remember."

With that Isabella walked over to the fire, threw in a handful of herbs and spoke softly to the flames. "Watch this fire, watch its light, help us to relive that night." As she did an image began to appear in the flames, everyone stared at the fire.

Chapter Fifteen
Time to prepare

As Nanny, Jess and the three cousins walked back to Nanny's house, the sun was starting to come up.

Nobody spoke and Nanny and Jess each had an arm around Mark's shoulders. Gypsy, Benjy and Flossy all walked quietly behind.

It had been a long night and Isabella had explained in great detail all about the night that Silas had come for the sun stone, how close he had come to assuming the full power of the Darach Nua and how Isabella had been forced to cast the spell that had left the world without Darach Nua for thirteen hundred years. A spell that would be lifted in twenty-four hours when the three cousins received their powers.

They had twenty-four hours to prepare for the ceremony and for what would happen, and for what could happen. Isabella had explained that although when the spell was lifted at the cousins' ceremony, Silas, Sean and Rowan would be mere mortals in this time as their powers were passed onto the cousins. Isabella did not know if Silas had the ability to travel back to that night. If he did, he would remember it better than anyone, and he would try everything to change the outcome in his own favour.

If this were to happen, they would all have to go back. Isabella, Roisin, Mark, Elliott and the guardians and defeat him once and for all.

Today they needed to prepare for the ceremony, but first they needed sleep, especially Mark. The group walked silently towards the gateway that led to the lane behind Nanny's house. As Elliott unlocked the gate the sound of thundering hooves could be heard. They all turned quickly to see where the sound was coming from. Gypsy and Benjy were barking furiously and as they looked towards where the sound was coming from. The black stallion, Silas, was charging towards them from the top paddock. Close on his heels were the two bay horses, Sean and Rowan.

"Mammy, get Mark through the gateway, Elliott, Roisin go with

Nanny quickly." Jess shouted frantically at Nanny and then stood there with her arms out to protect her wards, the dogs stood their ground, even Flossy, directly in front of Jess barking loudly and snapping at the air. As Silas the stallion thundered towards them, Sean and Rowan overtook him on either side and placed themselves between Jess, the barking dogs and Silas. They reared up on their hind legs, neighing loudly and snorting through their noses. This gave Jess enough time to get the dogs on the other side of the gateway and lock it.

"Thank you, Sean, thank you, Rowan," Jess called over her shoulder as she ran to catch up with the others. She was unsure if the horses could understand her, but given how protective they were, she was sure they could.

"We need to be careful now, Silas is very angry and he will try and get to Mark in any way he can before the ceremony; maybe he should stay home while we prepare for tomorrow."

Jess wrapped her arm around Mark's shoulders as she spoke, she felt the need to protect him, now more than ever.

"Agreed," replied Nanny. "I will stay with Mark today at the house, he's safe there while you three make the preparations. This ceremony cannot come soon enough. I will be so much happier when I know my squirrels have the power to protect themselves."

With that, they all hurried back to Nanny's house, just in time as it happened as Shiona was packing the car to go back to Ireland. "Where have you all been? You must have gone out very early? And what's wrong with Mark?" Shiona asked.

"Mark's fine, sweetheart, I think he's getting a summer cold. Jess you take Mark up to bed. We all went for an early morning walk to see the horses but Mark started to feel unwell so we came home." Nanny chatted away to Shiona as she continued to pack the car.

"Are you taking Kairen home, or is she getting the train?"

"I'm here, Mother," Kairen chirped in, coming down the stairs with a towel on her head. "Shiona is going to drop me at the train station when she heads for the ferry, we will be leaving in about an hour."

"Then I better get some breakfast on, can't have my girls travelling on an empty stomach." Nanny turned to walk back into the house, Roisin and Elliott stood there, mouths open. They were quite shocked that

Nanny was such a cool operator and so good at lying! She winked as she walked past them into the house. "You coming, my squirrels? You must have worked up quite an appetite."

They all enjoyed breakfast around the kitchen table and chatted as if this was an ordinary summer day.

With breakfast finished and a few tearful goodbyes, Shiona and Kairen set off to go to their respective homes, Shiona to Ireland and Kairen to Leeds.

When the goodbyes had finished and the frantic waving had stopped, Nanny ushered everyone back into the house. She closed the front door and then stayed there for a moment leaning on it with her back to the door.

"Nanny, are you OK?" asked Roisin. "Do you need to sit down?" Roisin seemed quite concerned about Nanny.

"Sit down?" laughed Nanny. "We don't have time to sit down, it's your ceremony tonight, let me check on Mark and then we will have a meeting in the kitchen." Nanny went up the stairs to check on the patient.

Nanny peeped around the bedroom door and Mark was fast asleep in the bottom bunk. The best place for him with all this happening Nanny thought to herself and closed the door quietly.

They all gathered around the kitchen table as Nanny had requested. "Come on, Nanny, what's the plan?" asked Elliott unable to wait any longer to find out what was happening.

"The first thing we need to do is complete the blessing passage, it hasn't been used in thirteen hundred years but it's still there. You will need to clear the steps of rocks and debris and find as many wild flowers as you can to decorate it. This will be a rite of passage for each of you.

"Jess, you will need to go with them and stay alert, Silas will know the time is drawing near. He won't be able to get to you in the bottom paddock beside Goderich brook, those fences are higher for a reason. Isabella knew this day would come. Before you start, Jessica, you must surround the passage with a circle of salt. Elliott, be sure to wear your amulet so you have the guardians to watch over you and Roisin; listen to your heart, you are close to receiving your power, your body is in tune with nature and you will be surprised how alert your intuitions have become. Work quickly this needs to be completed before midday."

"What will you do, Nanny?" asked Roisin.

"I will be here with Mark, I need to help him to be ready for this evening. He is weak now, but it will be a different story tonight. Silas will wish he had never heard of our Mark O'Neill, or indeed any of us."

"What will it be like, Nanny? When we get our powers, during the ceremony?" asked Roisin.

"I only know what Isabella has told me, and I promise you have nothing to worry about. As I said it is a rite of passage. Those who are lucky enough to have the opportunity to walk through the blessing passage are never the same when they come out the other side, their names are recorded in the Book of Time from then until eternity. The passage itself is a walkway dug into the earth, creating a channel to allow the air to pass through, it will be lined on either side with fires and it ends in front of Goderich Brook. During the celebrations just before sunrise, fires will be lit to line the passage and as you all, the Darach Nua, walk through the passage in the earth with the air travelling around you and the fires burning on either side you will be touched by the elements themselves. To complete the ritual you will be baptised in Goderich brook. I don't know how you will feel when you receive your powers, or indeed, my squirrels, if you will feel anything at all. I have no powers, but what I do know, is that this will be like no other blessing ceremony before. Sean and Rowan were the last to share a ceremony as they are twins, but there has never been three Darach Nua, the complete tri power all blessed together in the history of time. Or at least, that is what Isabella has told me."

"We had better go," said Jess, getting up to leave the table. "Shall we take the dogs?" she asked.

"Better leave Flossy here, if you have to run for it her little legs will slow you down," said Nanny, Jess might be twenty-one but the look her mother gave her meant this point was not up for discussion.

"You know best, Mammy," Jess replied smiling.

"One more thing and this is very important, when you are done, call up to Widdershins and ask Isabella if she has the dried immortelle for Mark's tonic for this evening, please don't forget."

With that Jess, Roisin, Elliott and the two dogs set off to prepare the passage. As they walked up the lane towards the bottom paddock, they could see the three horses in the top paddock looking down towards them. Jess could see Roisin appeared worried as she looked over.

"Don't worry, Roisin, they can't get down here, the fence is too high."

"I wasn't worrying about them coming down to us, I just felt super sad when I looked at Rowan. She has been trapped as a horse for thirteen hundred years, and it wasn't even her fault, all this because her brother was so bad. I can't imagine having a brother like that. I trust my brother with my life," said Roisin.

"So does Rowan," replied Jess. "Don't forget she has two brothers, Sean would protect her with his life. Tonight will be their freedom, but they won't be who they were, as they have lost their powers so it will be difficult for them, but they are not angry with you. When you become Darach Nua you know that you must do what is for the good of the earth and not for yourself. Sean, Rowan and Silas are now Darach Sean, remember Isabella explained it, Sean is the old Celtic word for old, the Darach Sean are the old Darach Nua with no powers."

"Will Silas really have no powers when he turns back into a man?" asked Elliott.

"That is the million-dollar question," replied Jess. "He won't have any of his given powers by the Darach Nua, but no one fully knows his relationship with the Underworld, we don't know if he was gifted powers from them that he will still have or if he will be totally mortal, that, my beautiful nephew and niece, is the reason we have to be so careful. The other thing we don't know is what powers you will be gifted, what will you get or how many will you get?"

"How many?" asked Roisin. "I thought we got one each?"

"In the old days each Darach Nua received one gift on their thirteenth birthday, they were most powerful when all three had come of age, but there have been no gifts and no Darach Nua for thirteen hundred years and as Nanny said, there has never been three Darach Nua gifted at the same time. So, will you receive a gift each or will you receive thirteen hundred years of unclaimed gifts?" Jess looked at Roisin and Elliott to try and judge their reaction to this news.

"What?" Elliott almost shouted his question. "We could be receiving thirteen hundred years' worth of back dated power? How long does a normal Darach Nua live? How many generations has it missed? I'm just trying to work out exactly how many gifts that would be?"

"Always asking questions and looking for answers aren't you, Elliott" said Jess.

"There is no time limit, as long as the three are healthy and wise the Darach Nua keep their power and grow wise, but if something happens to one, you all lose your powers and you become Darach Sean, like Sean and Rowan."

"Jess" said Roisin.

"Yes, Roisin," replied Jess.

"If we were to receive all the powers from the last thirteen hundred years, would it be safe? Will it hurt?" Roisin looked worried.

"Of course it won't hurt, I have never received powers and never will but what I do know is that Nanny and Isabella would protect you with their lives, there is no way they would do anything that would hurt you. Now come on, we need to clear these branches and stones from the steps, you would have hardly known this passage was here a few years ago. Isabella has been clearing it for so long, I believe, Elliott, that she was clearing it the day you met!"

They all set about carrying rocks and branches from the steps in the passage and placing them against the fence out of the way. It wasn't much of a passage any more, thirteen hundred years had taken its toll.

"I wish we had more time," said Elliott.

"I know I could excavate the earth and redefine the steps beautifully with a little more time. Nanny got me an archaeologist kit last year it would be perfect for this."

"You can always work on it again to bring it back to what it was, hopefully we are entering a new era and we will have more things to celebrate down here," said Jess.

"More things like what?" asked Roisin. "More Darach Nua?"

"Noooo, hopefully there will be no need for any more Darach Nua for a long time, but as you bring back the balance of nature, we will have nature's celebrations to enjoy," Jess laughed as she replied.

As the steps were now clear they stepped out of the passage and looked at their handiwork. "Flowers!" said Roisin.

"Of course," replied Jess. "And you know what? I think we should collect them from Widdershins, that way we can pick up the immortelle for Nanny too and we can decorate the passage on the way back."

"Sounds good to me," said Elliott.

"Buts it's already eleven a.m. so we better hurry, Nanny said it had to be complete by midday which I am guessing is twelve noon."

"Remember, stay alert, as we go towards the top paddock, Silas will know we are close." Roisin and Elliott looked at each other with concern.

"I wish Mark was here," said Roisin.

"Don't worry, Roisin, I will protect you," said Elliott and he put his arm around his cousin's shoulder to comfort her.

"Mark's fine, Roisin, I would know if something was wrong." Jess smiled at Roisin trying to comfort her, for brother and sister they were very close, almost like twins. They made their way to Widdershins each of them looking around and checking every sound they heard. As they approached the garden gate they heard Silas, as they turned around he was on top of the hill rearing up on his back legs and neighing at the top of his voice.

"Come on let's get inside quickly," said Roisin.

"He's already angry we don't want to make him worse.

The three of them hurried up the path and knocked on the door. Isabella opened the door and welcomed them in. "Benjy, Gypsy, stay outside we need you to keep guard."

Benjy and Gypsy seemed to know what was required and immediately went and sat at the gateway.

As they made their way into the kitchen, Isabella handed a pouch to Jess. "It's for your mother, immortelle for Mark."

"How did you know?" asked Jess but Isabella just smiled at her.

"Come sit at the table I have a few things for you before you collect your flowers." Elliott and Roisin looked at each other, how did she always seem to know everything?

"I won't see you again today until the ceremony as I have my own preparations to complete, you need to meet us down at the passage at nine o'clock, then we can finally redress the balance.

"Elliott, ensure you wear your amulet, you were given that for a reason and you won't know what it is until you need it. Roisin, wear this necklace."

Isabella tied a triquetra on a black leather cord around Roisin's neck.

"You are the centre of the Darach Nua, this necklace will help you to balance the power of three. Jess, you must be very careful tonight, you may not be receiving powers but Silas will know you are their Watcher and he will harm anyone who helps them given the chance. Take my white athame to cut the flowers, that way they will be blessed, bring the athame to the ceremony tonight, I will need it. Now go, be safe and be confident, you have all been chosen for a reason." Isabella got up from the table and opened the door. "Go now, be safe."

They all went out to the garden and Jess used the athame to cut roses and sweet peas by the armful, Roisin and Elliott's arms were overloaded.

"Jess, I think we have enough," said Elliott from behind a giant bunch of sweet peas.

"Ha-ha I think you may be right! Come on let's get back to the bottom paddock as quickly as we can, then we can get home to Nanny and Mark."

Gypsy and Benjy split up, Gypsy led them down the hill and Benjy followed behind watching the rear. They made it back to the bottom paddock without incident and arranged the flowers in and around the passage.

"Oh my, it looks beautiful," said Elliott. "But what's that?" Elliott ran over to the far side of the passage beside Goderich brook, there was a carved black handle sticking out of the ground. He brushed away the earth and tugged at it but it was stuck between tree roots. He tugged hard and with one final effort, it came loose. "It's a walking stick," said Elliott brushing the dirt from it. "Can I keep it?" he asked looking at Jess.

"You can for the moment, but it might belong to Isabella so we will check with her tonight."

Elliott was delighted with his new find and began to walk as though he were hiking through mountains with his new walking stick.

"Come on, you two, we are done here for now, let's get back and help Nanny."

Jess gathered up her helpers and called the dogs to heel and they all headed back to Nanny's house.

Chapter Sixteen
The ceremony

Mark sipped the immortelle tea Nanny had prepared and he was surprised how sweet it tasted. "Nanny, this is delicious," he said between sips. "It's so sweet I think I can actually feel my strength coming back as I sip it."

"Make sure you drink it all, I have put some in a flask to take to the ceremony, after that you shouldn't need it, but better safe than sorry if Silas is around," said Nanny.

"Nanny, if it's better safe than sorry should Elliott and I drink some? Just in case Silas sucks the strength out of us too?" asked Roisin.

Nanny laughed. "Silas isn't sucking the strength out of anyone, he's trying to draw energy, Mark isn't thirteen yet and will be the youngest Darach Nua ever, or so Isabella tells me. We don't think he will try with you too, but as I said, I have some in a flask just in case." Nanny winked at Roisin.

"I have to admit I'm quite nervous, in fact I think I might be sick," Elliott announced looking rather green and sheepish.

Nanny walked over to Elliott and put her hands on his shoulders, "Elliott Robb, you are one of the bravest and most intelligent young men I know, you have nothing to fear, tonight will be tremendous and things will never be the same again. If you were not nervous of the unknown I would be worried. Listen to me, my squirrels."

Nanny turned to face the three of them as they sat around the dining table and put her arm around Jess's shoulder to pull her in close. "Me and Auntie Jess will be there, Isabella and the guardians will be there, Benjy, Gypsy and Flossy will be there."

Nanny smiled as she said Flossy and looked over at the little bundle of fluffy fur curled up on the floor.

"We are going to make sure nothing happens to you, and to be honest, I get the feeling that after tonight, you won't need looking after and it will be you three taking care of us."

The three cousins were listening intently to every word. As Nanny finished speaking they looked at each other and all nodded in unison as though agreeing to this course of action.

"Now, we had better make a move, we promised Isabella we would be there for nine and its already twenty to."

Everyone stood up and prepared to leave.

"Last check," said Nanny. "Elliott, are you wearing your amulet?"

"Yes, Nanny." Elliott replied touching the amulet as he spoke.

"Roisin, are you wearing your triquetra that Isabella gave you?"

"Yes, Nanny," replied Roisin touching the triquetra as she spoke.

"Mark, have you finished your tea?"

"Yes, Nanny," replied Mark.

"Excellent, then we can go, oh I almost forgot, Jess, do you have Isabella's athame?

"Yes, Nanny," replied Jess mimicking her nephews and niece. They all laughed at this.

As Nanny opened the door, she held up her hand to stop them in their tracks. "Nanny, you remind me of Isabella when you do that," commented Roisin.

"I agree," said Elliott. "In fact, Nanny, you are reminding me of Isabella a lot lately."

"No changing the subject, young man. I stopped you for a reason, do you really need to bring that walking stick?" Nanny pointed to the stick Elliott had found earlier that day.

"Yes, Nanny. I found it on Isabella's farm and I want to ask if it's hers or if I can keep it."

"Fine, if you must, it's no harm I suppose," replied Nanny and ushered everyone including the dogs out of the kitchen through the back door.

Nanny and Jess led the way with the three cousins linking arms walking behind. As they approached the gateway to Widdershins Nanny stopped. "What is it Mammy?" asked Jess.

"The stone on the wall, I have never seen that before?" Nanny pointed to the rock that Elliott had found.

"I found it, Nanny, or at least it found me. I tripped over it the day

Mark and Roisin arrived, and then when I found out the farm used to be called Widdershins and not just Shins I showed Mark and Roisin. Mark lifted it onto the wall for us," Elliott explained.

"Nanny, what is Widdershin? I have heard it now a few times and not just about the farm?" Elliott asked.

"Widdershin is a very old word, it means in the opposite direction of the sun, or anticlockwise; sometimes a circle is cast Widdershin to deal with reversing things I think, Isabella would probably add a great deal to that explanation."

As if on cue, Isabella appeared around the corner of the field, waving and calling to Nanny. The three cousins ran over to Isabella and waited with her while Nanny and Jess caught up. The dogs were running around and barking, the air felt electric and the dogs knew something was in the air.

"Where are the guardians Isabella?" asked Roisin.

"We have to call them before they can attend the ceremony. Jess, do you have my athame?" Isabella asked.

"Of course." Jess pulled the athame from her shoulder bag and passed it to Isabella, holding it with two hands, one at the hilt and one carefully at the blade.

"Then let us begin." With that Isabella walked towards the blessing passage, it looked resplendent now in the evening sun with the sweet peas and roses decorating it.

Isabella walked the circumference of the blessing passage sprinkling salt as she did, muttering almost under her breath. "Hear me now and hear me true, through the passage of time I'm talking to you. Round and round the circles cast, joining present, future, past."

As Isabella walked the newly created salt circle, a hush started to descend around them, the leaves of the giant western oak seemed to freeze in time, no movement was in the air.

The cousins, Nanny and Jess looked on in awe and anticipation.

Isabella walked down the steps into the passage; she held her white handled athame into the air and began to call the guardians. "Guardian of the Eastern tower, guard this circle with your power, power of air I call this night, protect this circle with all your might."

As Isabella lowered her athame, a tall figure walked around the blessing passage and took up position at the eastern point and the air whipped around the blessing passage.

Isabella again raised her athame. "Guardian of the Southern tower, guard this circle with your power, power of fire I call this night, protect this circle with all your might."

As Isabella lowered her athame a second figure appeared beside the passage and took up position at the Southern point. As he did fires sprung up around the circle creating an impressive ring of fire.

Again, Isabella raised her athame. "Guardian of the Western tower, guard this circle with your power, power of water I call this night, protect this circle with all your might."

Mark nudged Roisin as Siar appeared at the western point of the circle. "It's Siar, he's here." Mark took Roisin's hand and squeezed it.

As Siar took his position Goderich brook swelled before their eyes and a wave flowed down the brook like a rapid and for a moment filled the passage.

For the final time Isabella raised her athame. "Guardian of the Northern tower, guard this circle with your power, power of earth I call this night, guard this circle with all your might."

This time it was Elliott who spoke. "It's Tuath, he's here."

Elliott took Roisin's hand and the three cousins stood hand in hand within the circle at the edge of the passage.

As Tuath took his position, the earth on the steps of the passage fell away revealing them as they had been thirteen hundred years before, beautifully sculpted into the earth.

Roisin, Mark and Elliott stood wide eyed staring at the passage, as the guardians now stood around it, Isabella within it and the power of the elements all around it was truly a sight to behold.

The flames danced around the circle as the wind spun around them almost like a mini tornado. The water lapped in and out of a small pool at the end of the blessing passage that had been transformed to its former glory, beautiful carved steps winding down at one end and narrowing to a small platform leading into the blessing pool at the other end filling from Goderich brook.

The cousins all held hands, Roisin in the middle with Mark and Elliott each squeezing one of her hands, as though in tune they all turned to look at Nanny and Jess at the same time. As they looked over, Nanny smiled, her warm comforting smile that said don't worry, everything is OK. Jess gave them the thumbs up and had a beaming smile, Gypsy, Benjy and Flossy all lay at the top of the steps waiting.

"It is time," said Isabella beckoning the three cousins into the passage. Together they walked down the steps and stood in the middle of the passage.

Roisin thought her heart might burst right out of her chest it was beating so hard. As she looked at Mark, as tall as he was, he looked small and afraid. She again squeezed his hand, unsure whether this was to comfort herself or to comfort Mark. As she looked at Elliott, his curls were sweaty and stuck to his face and he looked pale. In an effort to comfort Elliott, Roisin reached over and took his other hand, joining it with Mark's and completing the circle.

The moment the circle completed the flames jumped up into the air several feet, the power of the wind increased to the point that you could barely hear and Isabella held her hands high in the sky.

"Blood moon, solstice night. Anoint the Darach Nua tonight. Transfer the power that through time has slept. Heal the scars that the world has wept."

The air was electric and heavy, there was a loud thunderous sound, the three cousins turned around to look at Nanny as the thunder approached. It was then they realised it was not thunder, but horses' hooves, thundering down the field.

"Quickly, we must complete the blessing, Silas is here."

As Isabella spoke, the black stallion could be seen outside the circle, rearing up and the sound he made was terrifying. The bay horses were there too but they were silent and motionless, standing watching and waiting.

Isabella led the cousins to the pool at the end of the passage, as they stepped into the pool, they could see the sun stone in the bottom, it was as though light shone out of the stone itself, etched with strange letters and drawings.

"You must each fully immerse your heads, stay holding hands and do this now."

The cousins looked at each other, Roisin was the first to speak. "We have come this far together, we will do it on three."

Mark and Elliott nodded.

Together they counted. "One, two," as they all said the word "three" they took a deep breath and lay down in the pool. Light shone out of the stone like a beacon, the fires leaped, the wind whipped and the ground trembled, the water receded leaving the three cousins sitting in no more than an inch of water. As they stood up and stepped out of the now shallow pool, the earth closed over the stone, it was as though it had never been there.

They were still holding hands, dripping wet. "Roisin, your eyes, said Mark.

"No, your eyes," said Elliott. "It's all our eyes!" said Roisin.

Their eyes were the brightest green, like emeralds sparkling in the sun.

"I don't feel any different," said Elliott, but before his cousins could reply they heard Nanny shout.

"Isabella, look out it's Silas!"

Isabella and the cousins turned quickly, they could see the black stallion running around the circle anti clockwise at high speed, his hooves thundered so loudly it was deafening.

"Isabella, what do we?" shouted Nanny.

"He's running Widdershins, he's undoing the circle!" shouted Isabella. "Quickly, we must get out of the passage."

With that Isabella led the way and they all ran up the steps to where Nanny and Jess were stood.

"Where did you get that cane?" Isabella asked Jess in horror. Nanny and Jess looked at each other and then the cane.

"Elliott found it in the passage, he wanted to keep it but he wanted to ask you first if it was yours," replied Jess confused.

"It's not mine, it belongs to Silas!" shouted Isabella.

Before anyone could understand what this meant the circle began to collapse.

"Guardians of the quarters, stay with us," shouted Isabella, but it was too late the circle was down and the guardians had gone,. They gathered together to face Silas, as they turned around the stallion reared ferociously onto his hind legs, and then silence.

Total silence.

The cousins stood in total disbelief as walking towards them were three strangers, strangers and yet they knew exactly who they were, Sean and Rowan walking hand in hand and Silas walking alone. The veil was lifted, they were human again, they were no longer Darach Nua, now they were the Darach Sean.

Silas stopped and looked directly at Isabella. "Hello, Mother"

"Mother?" shouted Mark unable to stop himself. "You are Silas's mother?" He looked to his cousins for reassurance that his shock was warranted, he felt slightly validated when he saw the look of horror on their faces.

Rowan and Sean stepped beside their mother, one on each side with their arms around her shoulders. Isabella gently kissed both of them on their forehead. "My children, welcome home." She then turned to look at Silas. "Jessica, the cane, give it to me," said Isabella.

Jessica did not have time to respond before Silas snatched the cane from her hand. He whirled around striking Isabella on the temple with the cane. She fell to the floor unconscious. As he did so he took the cane in his hand, the black poplar handle feeling so familiar to his touch after such a long separation.

He proceeded to tap the ground, an evil smile spread across his face. He looked at the cousins with a stare so cold they started to shiver. He then tapped the ground again with his cane and called, "Widdershin", and with that, he was gone, nothing remained in the place where he had stood.

Nanny was the first to move. "Isabella." She crouched down beside her old friend and checked her pulse. "She is breathing but she is unconscious, we need to get her inside before he comes back."

"Back from where, Nanny?" asked an almost frantic Elliott.

"I don't know," replied Nanny. "Isabella would know, her head's bleeding, we need to move her now."

Rowan stepped forward to speak, "Silas has gone Widdershins, he could come back at any time."

"But where is Widdershins?" asked Elliott, the concern for his old friend clear on his face.

Rowan and Sean replied together, "The past."

"Now is not the time for questions we need to move Isabella," Nanny insisted. She too looked quite worried for Isabella.

"Let me," Mark pushed forward and he appeared taller, broader, older in fact. He scooped Isabella up into his arms as though she were no heavier than a rag doll.

"Let's get her home."

Chapter Seventeen
The gifted

Elliott walked silently ahead, not speaking and staring at the ground.

"Nanny, I'm worried about Elliott," said Roisin as they all marched up the hill towards Isabella's.

"I know, my squirrel, I'm also worried about Elliott and Isabella," replied Nanny.

"I will go and try to talk to Elliott," stated Jess.

"He feels guilty about the walking stick, it's weighing him down, I can feel it like a lump in my chest."

"You can actually feel his feelings?" asked Nanny.

"Before it was like a thought or a feeling, but now I can physically feel it, I need to speak to him."

Jess and Flossy ran ahead and caught up with Elliott. Jess put her arm around Elliott's shoulder and gave him a squeeze. "Elliott, don't forget, I'm not only your aunt, but your Watcher, if you feel pain, I feel pain, if you are afraid or upset I can feel it. That way I can protect you when we are not together. Please don't blame yourself because of the walking stick, some things are written in time and are meant to be, this moment was always going to happen. How we deal with it is the important thing. Isabella would not want to see you giving in so soon because of this."

Elliott didn't reply he just kicked a stump of grass as he walked.

"Elliott, you're not alone, come here." Jess pulled him in closer and they continued the walk up the hill with their arms around each other's shoulders. Jess knew he was hurting but the longer they walked the lighter the weight in her chest felt, so she knew it was helping him, at least a little.

The group arrived at the top of the hill and walked down the small path that led to Isabella's garden. As Elliott reached out his hand to open the gate, the gate opened before he could touch it.

"Did you see that?" Elliott asked Jess.

"I did, was it you, or was it the wind?"

Jess stopped and held out her hand. There was not a breath of air, the night was completely still.

"I think it was me?" Elliott said and all the colour had drained from his face.

"Don't be afraid, we knew you would receive a gift of power, maybe this is it?"

"Great! I can open gates with a wave of the hand," Elliott replied sarcastically. Jess let this comment pass as she knew he was struggling to control his feelings.

They walked up the path and again as Elliott reached for the door, before he touched the handle, it opened.

"Well that's my power covered, not quite what I expected but hey, at least I will be the world's greatest porter!" Elliott laughed at this, Jess joined in and for a moment, it seemed as though the tension had passed.

Everyone was now back at the farmhouse. Mark lay Isabella on the window seat, the same one that he had lay on only the night before, only a night but yet he felt like it was a lifetime. He felt stronger and somehow wiser and he was definitely a little bigger. He picked up the patchwork blanket from the back of Isabella's chair and covered her over with it.

It was strange to see Rowan and Sean in the kitchen, they were clearly home, their home. Rowan filled the kettle and reached for the cups, knowing where everything was without needing to ask. Sean the same, he disappeared into another room and returned with spare chairs that he placed around the table. He then began to stoke the fire and went outside to collect wood from the yard.

For the first time since the ceremony Roisin, Mark and Elliott were alone as they sat at the table, the three of them joined hands for comfort as they watched Nanny and Jess tend to Isabella.

Elliott could wait no more. "I can open things."

"What?" asked Mark puzzled. "We can all open things."

"Yes, but can you open things without touching them?"

"Of course not," replied Mark.

"Exactly," replied Elliott. "I think that's my power, watch..."

He walked over to the door and reached for the handle, before he touched it, the door swung open into his hands.

"Wow," said Mark. "That's amazing, just doors? or locked doors?" asked Mark.

"Let's see," said Elliott.

He closed the door to the kitchen and turned the key. As he stood back and reached for the handle the key turned in the lock and the door swung open into his hands.

"Elliott, that's amazing, is it just doors, well, locked doors or do you have telekinesis?" asked Roisin.

"Tele ken what?" asked Mark.

"It's where you think about things moving in your mind, and they just do it, remember we saw that scary film where that man could do it," Roisin added.

"Yes, I remember, the scary one we watched with Jess, where they all wore flares and had big collars. Wow that was an old film, but a good one. Try it, Elliott, come sit at the table and see can you move something like a spoon."

Elliott did as he was told and sat down.

"Try this," said Mark, pushing one of Isabella's silver spoons towards him. "Stare at it and tell it to move in your head."

"He means, will it to move with your thoughts, without touching it, maybe put your hands on your temples, like this, that's what he did in the movie." Roisin placed her hands on her temples to show Elliott what she was trying to explain.

"I know you are, I'm only trying to help," Roisin replied to Elliott. "What?" said Elliott. "I didn't speak."

"You did I heard you, you said what do you think I'm doing?"

"No, I didn't," retorted Elliott.

"You did I heard you and Mark did too, Mark tell him."

Roisin looked at her brother to back her up, Mark just looked at her blankly. "Roisin, Elliott didn't say a word," replied Mark gently. "Are you OK?"

"But, but I definitely heard him," protested Roisin. "Roisin." Roisin turned around quickly and Rowan was stood behind her. "Roisin, you can hear me can't you."

"Of course I can hear you?" Roisin replied to Rowan. "Roisin, look at me, carefully. I am not speaking."

"Of course you are speaking, I can hear you, we can all hear you."

Roisin looked to Mark and Elliott who were now sitting staring at Roisin, eyes wide. "Roisin, why are you shouting at Rowan, she hasn't said a word?"

Rowan sat in the chair beside Roisin and took her hand. "Roisin, it is thoughts you are hearing not words, you have the gift of truth, it will take time but you will be able to control your power, you can choose to see or hear the truth. Just like Elliott, you need to focus your powers and train them as Sean and I did when it was our time."

Rowan stroked Roisin's hair and got up from the table leaving the cousins alone again. The cousins sat in stunned silence.

"Well that is you and me sorted, what about Mark?" asked Elliott.

"I actually think Mark looks older and taller already," said Roisin meekly, clearly shaken by what had just happened.

Mark stood up and looked himself up and down as much as it is possible to look yourself up and down. "To be honest, I feel different. I feel, well, kind of calm and in control, and I'm not afraid, actually not afraid of anything any more. Not even of getting powers, or Silas, but I am worried about Isabella."

The three cousins looked over to where Nanny and Jess were still tending to Isabella. "Mark, help us lift Isabella, we need to sit her up so we can try and give her some of the immortelle tea in Nanny's flask."

Jess had barely finished her sentence and Mark was beside her. "Flippen eck! Did you see that?" shouted Elliott! Elliott jumped up from his seat knocking his cup over onto the floor. "He actually just, well he transported across the room! There is no other way to describe it!"

He bent down to pick his broken cup up and as he did, he cut his hand. "Ouch!" he cried out as the blood trickled from the cut in his palm.

Jess was instantly beside him and took a tissue from her pocket to cover the wound and pressed it to stop the bleeding.

"Flippen 'eck! Jess can do it too! You just transported over here!"

"Did I?" said Jess looking as shocked as Elliott sounded,

"I just saw you were hurt and needed to get to you."

She removed the blood-soaked tissue to check the wound. "Elliott? Look what you did?"

Elliott and Jess looked at his hand where the tissue had been and there was nothing there, no cut, no blood, just a bloody tissue.

"I err I don't know," said Elliott, looking very shocked, the colour drained from his face.

"Jess, Elliott needs to sit down he's going to..." before Roisin could finish her sentence Elliott fainted.

"Roisin, you knew that was going to happen didn't you?" asked Mark.

"No, Elliott said he thought he was going to faint, or at least I thought he said it."

"Please, Jess, squirrels, we need to help Isabella" Nanny spoke quite sternly. "We can sit down together soon, but, for now Isabella is our priority. Jess, make sure Elliott is OK, he's only fainted from the blood he's a strong young man."

Jess stroked Elliott's curls away from his face and he was already waking up. "Are you OK, you fainted?"

Elliott jumped to his feet a little embarrassed that he had fainted, "Of course I am, I am Darach Nua," and he gave Jess a beaming smile that showed that he was definitely more than OK. "I'm just not good with blood, especially mine, or lack of blood for that matter."

Mark lifted Isabella gently and Nanny propped her up with cushions, covering her over again when she seemed to be in a comfortable position on the window seat, but she was still out cold.

"Nanny, can I try, I might have just fixed my hand, maybe I can fix Isabella's head." Elliott looked desperate to help Isabella and Nanny could see this.

"Of course, just be gentle." Nanny moved away from Isabella's side and allowed Elliott to move in close. He placed his hand on her temple where the blood had now dried. He held it there for a moment and then removed his hand, hoping beyond hope that it would be the same as his hand. As he removed his hand, his disappointment was clear, there was no change.

"Jess, you must try, it must have been you that healed my hand," Elliott insisted.

"But, Elliott, I don't have powers, I am not a Darach Nua," Jess replied, you could hear the sadness in her voice.

This time it was Sean who stepped forward, he took Jessie's hand and placed it on Isabella's forehead.

"You are a true Watcher now. Watchers do not only watch, where would be the benefit of that?" as he released Jessie's hand, Isabella started to move and the cut on her forehead was healed.

Jess smiled at Sean, and then looked at Nanny, the smile on Jessica's face spoke volumes. "I don't understand? How? Why can I do that?" Jess asked Sean.

"You are a Watcher now, and a healer, there will be times when only you can save them, nature bestows gifts for a reason, to keep the balance, these are the gifts nature has chosen for you."

"And the transporting?" Jess asked,

"I have never heard that word before so I do not know, but when you move through time quickly, as you did to Elliott, that is called Deosil, moving forward in time in the direction of the sun, as Silas went Widdershins, the reverse direction of the sun, you went Deosil."

Isabella started to mumble, "Silas, Silas, the cane."

Nanny wiped Isabella's forehead and lifted the tea to her lips. She was only able to wet Isabella's lips with the tea, but even that small amount seemed to work.

Isabella looked around the room frantically as though she had lost something. Her eyes stopped when she came to Rowan and Sean, her whole demeanour softened and she held out her arms. Rowan and Sean knelt before their mother and she closed her arms around them.

"We will let you catch up," Nanny said and gave Jess the eyes that meant follow me. They all sat at the table leaving Isabella with Sean and Rowan at the window seat.

"Nanny, are you crying or do you have something in both your eyes?" Mark asked smiling. It was true Nanny's eyes were glassy as though she were about to cry.

"You little tinker," she replied to Mark. "It just melts me to think of how happy they must be right now. I can't imagine the pain of being separated from my children, or grandchildren for that matter, not for thirteen days never mind thirteen hundred years."

They all looked over to the window seat where Isabella, Sean and Rowan were still hugging each other and the joy on their faces was clear to see.

"Right, my squirrels, where are we up to this night? You are discovering your gifted power; I think you better tell me exactly what is going on. Jess can you pour the tea and Mark, could you get some biscuits please." Nanny pointed in the direction of the tea and the biscuits.

"Elliott, could you get a fresh cup please it appears you have broken yours." Elliott looked sheepishly at Nanny and stood up from the table. As he did Nanny took his hand. "Elliott, I hope that you don't blame yourself in any way for this evening, much of life is mapped out in destiny and we are only players in the game. Very few among us are lucky enough to have an opportunity to change things and improve the course of time for everyone, you are one of those people. Don't let the beauty and importance of what has happened to you tonight to become lost in regrets of something that Silas planned thirteen hundred years ago. That is his to endure, not yours."

Elliott wasn't sure why but he felt instantly comforted by Nanny's words, he knew she was right.

Silas had planned all along to retrieve his cane and gain revenge; there was nothing Elliott could have done before to change this.

Elliott returned with his cup and spoke softly to Nanny, almost as though he didn't want anyone to hear. "Nanny, I don't know how but I am going to fix this, no, we are going to fix this. I couldn't before, we couldn't before, but we are Darach Nua now, and Silas will pay for hurting Isabella, his own mother, how could he?"

"I know you will, and if I can I will help you. As for Silas, I just don't know, not everyone has a good heart like you, always remember that, but just because someone has darkness in their past it doesn't mean there will never be light in their future."

"Nanny, you sound more like Isabella every day," replied Elliott and now his smile had returned.

"Nanny," interrupted Roisin. "You know you asked us to tell you about our gifted powers, well it's not just us, Jess has them too."

"Is this true, Jessica?" Nanny asked Jess smiling.

Just as Jess was about to answer Roisin got up from the table. "Can I let the dogs in, Gypsy is cold, and it hurts her legs when she's lying on the stones outside."

"Of course," replied Nanny. "But how did..." Nanny stopped herself and smiled. "Of course, you can, what a wonderful gift to receive, although I think you could always communicate with the animals, even before tonight."

Nanny and Roisin smiled at each other, and they both knew she was right.

Jess returned to the table and explained to Nanny exactly how Sean had explained to her about Deosil and Widdershins.

"I saw you heal Isabella's head, but I had thought that was your calling as a Watcher, to watch and heal. Jess you must be delighted, but remember, you must be careful, you are always so quick to rush in to help anyone, you need to protect yourself too, you will be no help as a Watcher if you go flying through time and land in trouble you can't get out of. I know, I know, but I can't help but worry, you are still my little Jess no matter how big you get or how many gifts you receive."

"Don't worry, Mammy, I will be careful, I don't intend rushing through time anytime soon," laughed Jess and the others joined in with the laughter.

"And, my squirrels, what have you discovered this evening?" asked Nanny looking around the table at the faces smiling back at her. She couldn't help but notice how they were all looking so grown up, her little squirrels were not so little any more and she had to admit, even if only to herself, she was more than a little worried about what the future would hold now they were Darach Nua.

Roisin squeezed Nanny's arm. "You don't need to worry, Nanny."

"Hey, missy, no reading Nanny's thoughts," Nanny said gently.

"I didn't, I don't need to read your thoughts, actually, I'm not sure that I can even if I want to."

"Well that's good for me then," smiled Nanny.

They chatted for a while discussing the powers they had received, the longest day of the summer was coming to a close but the blood moon still lit up the sky outside like a lantern.

"Elliott, could you light more candles please, it's getting very dark in here," Nanny asked. Elliott didn't move from his seat but instead sat motionless with a strange look on his face.

"Elliott? Are you OK?" Nanny asked.

As she spoke the candles on the table lit up. "Haha! I did it! Did you see that! I lit the candles with my mind! I didn't even move a muscle except for my brain and the candles lit!"

Nanny clapped her hands. "What gifted little squirrels I have."

The momentary celebration was interrupted by Isabella calling order. "Mark, bring me to the fireplace, we need to see if time has changed."

Mark immediately got up from his seat and went over to assist Isabella. He lifted her as gently as you would lift a newborn and carried her to the sofa beside the fireplace.

Isabella called Nanny to her side. "I need you to help me, sit beside me and follow my instructions please, we need to check the flames, gather everyone around."

Everyone gathered on the sofa and the chairs beside the fireplace, Isabella took a handful of thyme out of her apron and passed it to Nanny. Isabelle whispered something in Nanny's ear and Nanny stood beside the fireplace as though she was waiting for something.

Isabella called for quiet in the room and when all eyes were on her she began to speak. "To fix the past the present we must heal. Lift the veil so the truth will reveal. Repair the damage the wounds in time. Return the balance so the guardians can align."

Nanny stepped forward and threw the thyme into the flames, the sparks crackled and the flames began to change colour. The flames parted and a room came into view.

As they all stared into the flames Isabella continued. "Watch the flames and the tale will tell, watch the flames and understand well."

The picture in the flames became clearer, it was a room, but not just any room, it was this room. The very kitchen they were all now sitting in, but it looked different. The table was still set with dirty dishes, but these were not the beautiful dishes that Isabella kept with such pride, they were odd unmatching, chipped dishes. The floor was dirty and unkept and you could barely see through the windows through the dirt and grime. Beside the front door was a staff, a walking stick, with a black poplar handle. Movement could be heard from the other side of the room and then Silas came into view.

He had a bunch of herbs in his hand and he carried them over to the table. He took an athame from his jacket to chop them, the athame was not his, it was Isabella's white athame that she had lent to Jess earlier that day. As he chopped the herbs, he recited the same words over and over again. "Thirteen hundred years for my will to bend, thirteen hundred years till Darach Nua's end."

As he spoke there was a knock at the kitchen door. Silas went to open it and before he did he smoothed his hair, fixed his clothing and a sickening, fake smile appeared on his face.

Silas swung open the door and greeted his guest with a beaming smile. "Elliott, my friend, I have been waiting for you."

"Sorry I'm late, my cousins are visiting from Ireland and I was helping Nanny, she loves the solstice."

"No need to apologise, my old friend. I hadn't forgotten, I have been waiting for this day too." As Silas turned away from Elliott the evil smirk returned to his face.

"You remembered what we agreed, Elliott, you must bring your cousins here this night, we can all celebrate the solstice together."

"Of course, how could I forget. I actually think you are more excited to meet them than I was," laughed Elliott.

"Not at all, my old friend, let's just say I have been waiting a long time to get you all together in one place, a long time."

As Silas spoke, he played with an amulet around his neck, it was a beautiful yellow amber on one side but on the reverse it was a black, smooth stone. As he stroked it he remembered the Seer, the day she had given him the black stone amulet and all that had been since. He turned around and spun on his heels. "Elliott, you had better return to your nanny's house, we don't want her to worry and I have many preparations to make. Tonight, will be very special, you have no idea."

As Elliott turned to leave, the flames crackled and the picture faded.

"Elliott, did you see that you were friends with Silas! Why would you? Why would you betray us?" Mark stood up with anger as he spoke.

Elliott had a look of horror on his face, the colour had drained and he stood up to face Mark to defend himself. As he stood in front of Mark now, it was clear how much bigger Mark had become in one night, nevertheless, Elliott stood his ground. "I am not friends with Silas, I have never been friends with Silas and I can tell you one thing for sure, Mark

O'Neill, I have no plans to be friends with him in the future!"

The colour had returned to Elliott's face and he was flushed with anger, he clenched his fists into tight balls and spun around to challenge anyone who disagreed with his last statement.

Isabella lifted her hand, it had the same effect as it had only a few days before, the room went silent, all eyes were on Isabella. "Elliott has betrayed no one and if we are careful, he will never be Silas's friend. That is not the truth you have seen tonight in the flames but a possible present. Silas must have gone back to re-live the final battle, and, I am very sorry to say, if, in his newly created future, he lives at Widdershins and is planning to meet the three of you for the solstice this night, it would appear he has won and I am no more, Sean and Rowan are no more, and from what I have just seen, what we all have just seen, he intends to make sure the next generation of Darach Nua is no more."

They all sat in stunned silence.

Jess spoke up first. "Isabella, you said *if* we are careful Elliott will never be Silas's friend. Does that mean we can stop his new future?"

"It does indeed," smiled Isabella. "It does indeed."

The cousins looked at Jess, then at Nanny and then everyone looked at Isabella.

"It is time to go back and address the balance, we must go back and protect the stone and stop Silas once and for all. He has the power of the Underworld with him. Did you see his amulet, it was Elliott's amulet with a stone from the Black Sea on the reverse. Gather around I have a plan, but we must act quickly before the sun comes up on a new day."

Chapter Eighteen
The gateway

As the unusual looking group marched through the half-darkness of night, across the fields towards Nanny's house, the blood moon was high in the sky. Not a word was spoken.

Mark carried Isabella and Rowan and Sean walked beside him. Nanny led the way with Jess and Elliott and Roisin walked silently behind; even the dogs were silent, padding along softly behind Roisin and Elliott in single file, first Gypsy, then Benjy and Flossy at the rear.

The plan of action had been decided by Isabella, or at least the possible plan of action had. She advised them strongly of the possible dangers of Widdershins, but if they were willing to take the risk, this was the only way to stop Silas from changing the past and in turn, all their futures. Isabella had been preparing for this eventuality for a long time as she had always known Silas would not let the past rest.

Nanny's house was the key, this was as much a surprise to Nanny as it had been to everyone else.

Isabella had explained that in the years after the veil, the land that had been Silas's home had been used for homesteads for the forest folk, many of them were now gone but Nanny's house was built on the outcrop of rock that Silas's cave had once been hollowed into. The giant apple tree in Nanny's garden had once stood in Silas's herbal garden. Isabella said that Nanny's house had been in the possession of the forest folk for thirteen hundred years, and only in the last few years had she come to realise that Nanny must be a true descendant of the old times.

The decision was that Roisin, Mark and Elliott would go Widdershins, Isabella could not go with them as she didn't want to meet herself in the past, not that she actually couldn't, but if she did it could have repercussions as she was the Keeper of Time and it could create a loop.

Roisin, Mark and Elliott would go back alone, they would need to

155

find the sunstone and bring it with them to the future to prevent any further threat in the past. That aside they would have the small matter of Silas to deal with.

Whatever Silas had done, he did it on the night of the solstice either in their own time or in the past, Isabella would fix it so that they arrived the morning of the solstice, this hopefully would give them time to find past Isabella and create a plan. Isabella gave Roisin a piece of brown folded paper with strict instructions to pass this to past Isabella upon meeting her.

Nanny was not happy with this plan, she was very concerned about the cousins travelling through time to a strange place whether they were Darach Nua or not. Isabella tried to reassure Nanny that all things were meant to be and the threads of time had already been cast, all they had to do was untangle them.

The Darach Nua were a strong force of nature in the past and from what Isabella had seen this night, they were much stronger in the present.

As they arrived at Nanny's they all gathered around the kitchen table. Isabella spoke calmly to the cousins. "You know what happened on this night in the past, you must find past me and give me my note, the veil will not fix this problem it will only repeat what has already happened. Make sure I understand this, you will need the help of the guardians and the forest folk. You have your powers now and maybe more that remain as yet undiscovered, do not be afraid to use them, but only ever use them for good or the three-fold law will apply and your gift will work against you times three.

"Remember you are each strong and powerful Darach Nua, but when you act as one your powers are increased three-fold, as long as you act with good in your hearts."

Isabella reached into her apron pocket and took out the six vials. She passed a red vial marked 2018 to Roisin, Mark and Elliott. "When it is time to return, drink this and think of home, this home and the gateway between the times should open." She placed the three green vials marked 718 onto the kitchen table. "To go Widdershins through the gateway, you must each drink this."

"But where is the gateway, Isabella, I have been here so many times and I have never seen a gateway?" asked Elliott.

"I have to be honest," added Nanny, "I have lived here for most of my life and neither have I."

"It's a gateway through the realms of time, it's always there but not just anyone can open it, you need to know the key," replied Isabella smiling.

"Do you have the key?" asked Roisin.

"Well if the Keeper of Time doesn't have the key I don't know who would," commented Mark.

"You are getting very sarcastic, little big brother," replied Roisin.

"Now, now, let's not lose our concentration. Yes of course I have the key," said Isabella quite sternly.

"The gateway is here in the kitchen, but as I said it hasn't been used for over thirteen hundred years, from my recollection of the old homestead that was here, it should be in the cupboard under the stairs."

Nanny and Jess looked at each other with surprise. Nanny had only redecorated under the stairs last month, newly painted walls and freshly laid tiles. Grandad had fitted it out with shelves to restore it to a pantry.

"I think I would have noticed a gateway when I decorated," Nanny added.

"It's a gateway that leads to Silas's cave, once opened it will lead down into the chosen time but always in that place. We will need to break out the floor to reveal the original seal; this I'm afraid will not be easy, and I apologise now as I think it may also be messy," said Isabella.

"Hold on just a moment, how are we supposed to break out a concrete floor, reveal a hidden gateway, travel to the past, fix the future and defeat Silas all in one night?" Elliott asked and he was not being sarcastic, he really wanted to know.

Isabella looked straight at Elliott and stated matter of factly, "That, my Darach Nua, is where you come in, and please focus because it would really please your nanny if you could do this without destroying her house."

All eyes were on Elliott.

"What? How can I do it, Mark is much stronger than I am," Elliott protested.

"You don't need my strength," replied Mark, "Use your mind."

Mark was smiling from ear to ear, he was clearly enjoying this new phase of being gifted and secretly enjoying Elliott's surprise at the thought of ripping up Nanny's floor in the middle of the night.

"Come on, Elliott, you can do it," encouraged Roisin.

"OK, don't rush me, I have only been doing this for, well, OK I'm totally new to this."

Elliott was now grinning too, he shook his arms and rolled his neck around as though he were preparing to lift a heavy object, then he settled his feet into fighting stance. He looked towards Mark and Roisin, still grinning and placed his fingers to his temples. They grinned back at him, each remembering their earlier conversation.

"Just to be clear, you want the whole floor taking out from under the stairs?" asked Elliott looking straight at Isabella.

"Yes, everything, you won't be able to move the original seal, only the Keeper of Time can do that."

Elliott turned back to face his challenge and squinted his eyes as he stared intently at the small pantry cupboard.

"Sorry, Nanny, about your floor I mean," he added still grinning profusely. The room was silent, waiting and watching.

Then it started, the sound was strange in the silence of the night. A crackling scratching sound, then it happened. The first tile flew up into the air. The smile on Elliott's face intensified, he jumped up and changed stance to face the opposite direction. "Don't worry, Nanny, I got this, I won't make a mess," he shouted laughing and clearly enjoying himself.

The tile flew to the far corner of the kitchen and settled neatly on the floor. Elliott again jumped and changed stance and another tile lifted. This continued until there was a neat little pile of removed tiles at the far side of the kitchen, under the stairs the bare concrete floor had been revealed.

"OK, I'm going to need space to do this bit cleanly, clear the way I need a path to the back door."

Elliott marched over to the back door as though he were a man on a mission, he assumed the fighting stance, placed his fingers on his temples and the wheelbarrow lifted up in the air from the bottom of the garden and moved to the back door. Elliott marched back to his position in front of the cupboard under the stairs. He assumed his now recognised position, fighting stance and fingers on his temples and again began to stare.

The room seem to grumble at the pressure Elliott was placing on it, but then piece by piece the concrete lifted clean out of the floor and moved through the air in single file landing gently in the wheelbarrow at the back door. Elliott turned to face his captive audience and bowed as though he were an actor who had just finished a scene on stage. The room filled with applause.

"I never doubted you for a moment," said Isabella smiling. As she did, she placed her hand on her chest and the colour in her face turned to grey.

"Isabella, are you OK?" Mark asked appearing at her side in a flash.

"It's Silas," said Isabella, "whatever he is doing in the past is starting to take effect here and now. We need to act quickly, I don't have long."

As the dust cleared under the stairs an old wooden door was revealed in the floor, it had thick black iron hinges and looked like the lid of a treasure chest.

"It's time to go," said Isabella. The group gathered around and all gave each other hugs.

Nanny gathered the cousins together and hugged all three of them at the same time. "Remember, my squirrels, if it is too dangerous or you are afraid, you haven't failed, just come home, we deal with what happens next together, you are the only thing that is important to me."

"To us," Jess added and joined the group hug. "I will be here and I will know if you need me, I'm not sure what I can do from here but I will do anything I can to help."

"Let's be honest," said Mark. "We're not really sure what we're going to do when we get there either." He smiled but his smile was a little unconvincing.

"Wait, I need my backpack." Mark ran up to the bedroom to retrieve it from the bottom of the wardrobe before hurtling back to the kitchen in record time.

"I don't think I will ever get used to seeing you move so fast," commented Elliott,."It's like a blur."

"I could say the same about your construction skills," laughed Mark.

"You mean his de-construction skills," laughed Roisin.

Isabella took the three green vials from the kitchen table and passed them to each of the cousins, "Drink this and when the gateway is open, your pathway will be before you."

The cousins looked at each and then around the room, then back to each other.

Isabella began to recite the words:

"Gateway to the past, true and fast.

Lessons to learn before you return.

Gateway to the past, true and fast.

Lessons to learn before you return"

As Isabella spoke the door in the floor creaked and opened revealing a dark stone stairway with fog lingering from around halfway down. A damp, stagnant smell travelled into the kitchen from the gateway and the temperature in the room dropped.

The cousins clinked together their little vials as though they were raising a toast. "Cheers," they all said in unison before drinking the contents of the 718 bottles.

"No point in waiting any longer," said Roisin, running ahead through the doorway and down the steps.

"No! Roisin, don't go through!" Mark called after his sister. He wasn't sure if she heard him, as she disappeared into the eerie fog he saw her turn around and reach out her hand.

"Mark," she called as she looked back over her shoulder, but her voice was so feint it was as though she was miles away in the distance and not simply at the bottom of the stairs.

"Elliott, we can't let her go alone, come on." Mark grabbed Elliott by the arm and pulled him towards the stairs, the fog was starting to clear but he couldn't see Roisin, just the cold stone floor of a cellar through an eerie almost iridescent blue fog.

"Jump," Mark shouted, and as he did his own voice sounded strange to his ears, like it was the voice of some-one else far away.

Mark felt the cold stone against his knees as he landed on the cellar floor. It was dark and his eyes tried to adjust to the lack of light. He felt a hand on his arm. "Elliott?"

"No, it's me," said Jess from behind Mark.

"What are you doing here? I thought Isabella said only the Darach Nua could go Widdershins?" asked Mark sounding clearly surprised but also relieved.

"I was worried one of you might need healing and I wouldn't be there, so I grabbed a vial from the table and drank it. You will have to share some of your red bottles with me if I am to travel back as well," Jess said smiling.

"I'm glad you are here," said Mark giving Jess a generous hug. "But where is Elliott? And Roisin?"

"I was behind Elliott and you were behind Roisin? We should all be together?" replied Jess puzzled.

"Has Elliott passed you on the stairs?"

"No, I had a hold of his arm when I jumped through the fog, and then you grabbed me?" Jess called to the missing cousins and waited for a reply.

As they listened and waited the sound of a door closing overhead left them in complete darkness.

"I guess that's the gateway closing for now, they must be on this side, we all came the same way," said Mark very matter of fact, but Jess could hear the concern in his voice.

"Let's stick together, I can't see a thing," said Jess squeezing Mark's arm.

"Hold on," Mark reached into his back pack and pulled out his Maglite. "I knew this would come in handy."

He flicked on the tiny torch and shone the light all around. As the light bounced off the walls they could see they were not really in a room as they would describe it as the walls were made of rock, dark, damp and uneven. Water trickled down the walls in places and there was a stench in the air.

"I have to admit, I don't really like the dark," said Jess.

"I have to admit I didn't really like it either, before, but it's not bothering me at all. What I am bothered about is the fact that we have half of our rescue party missing," replied Mark.

"Here, you hold the torch, Jess, my eyes are adjusting and I can see quite well, maybe it's another power."

As Mark turned to pass the torch to Jess, he heard footsteps on the stone stairs behind them. "Mark."

Mark and Jess spun around to see where the sound had come from, they could hear Rosin's voice on the stairs.

"Roisin, we are here!" Mark's voice was elated. "Is Elliott with you? Where have you been?"

"Where have we been?" replied Elliott clearly out of breath. "There must be a hundred steps in that passage and you two just, well, we need a name for it, you just blurred past us at the speed of light."

Mark and Jess looked at each other, they hadn't even realised that they had done it.

"We are sorry," said Jess, it's this new gift we have. We must have both 'blurred' without realising, I thought there was only a few steps."

"Me too," confirmed Mark. "I was really worried when you two weren't here, I didn't even realise we had passed you and left you behind."

"Our powers are becoming clearer, we are using them without realising," smiled Jess.

"We aren't cross, or at least I'm not, I can feel that you were worried, next time you two decide to 'blur', do us a favour and each grab one of us slow coaches, we might be able to tag along," said Roisin walking over to Mark and giving him a big hug.

"I agree with Roisin, next time you 'blur' I want to tag along," agreed Elliott. "Talking of tagging along, I had no idea you were joining us until you flew past Jess, welcome to the rescue party."

"I knew," Roisin said smiling knowingly. "She planned it as soon as Isabella placed the bottles on the table."

"Aren't we a gifted little group?" laughed Jess.

"Come on, back to business, if everything has gone to plan, we are somewhere around Silas's cave and for all we know he could be in it. We need to get out of here and find past Isabella."

"Agreed," repeated everyone else.

"I'll lead the way I have the torch," stated Jess and was about to set off.

"Actually I can see perfectly well in the dark," said Elliott.

"Me too," agreed Roisin.

"Aren't you the lucky ones," laughed Jess.

"I will lead the way, everyone behind me." Mark set off ahead and no one questioned his leadership as they all secretly felt a little safer with him up ahead.

The group set off from the bottom of the stairs and started to make their way along a tunnel. "Can you feel that? It's a breeze coming down this way, we must be getting close to the exit, wait here, I'll go ahead and see if it's safe."

Without waiting for agreement Mark blurred up ahead and retuned before anyone had the opportunity to question his decision.

"There is an exit up ahead it leads into a garden with a large apple tree."

As the light from the tunnel exit came into a view, Roisin suddenly stopped. "Wait," she said holding up her hands.

"What is it, Roisin?" asked Mark.

"We need to wait, there is someone in the garden outside," she replied.

"How can you tell?" asked Elliott.

"The crow told me, wait he's coming in, the crow I mean not the person in the garden."

Just as Roisin had said a large black glossy crow flew into the tunnel. It opened its wings in readiness to land and as his wings fluttered and there was a flurry of jet black cloth and the wings were no more but instead there stood a young striking man, clothed in a rich black cape with hair as black as that of the crow's feathers. His face was pale and white with a very angular nose and his eyes were piercing yellow, bathed with thick black lashes.

The young man took his cape in one hand and bowed down before Roisin. "My lady, Roisin, we finally meet, in person."

He reached out his hand and took Roisin's in his, placing a gentle kiss on the back of her hand as he continued to bow.

Roisin blushed at his chivalry. "My friend, it is good to finally meet you too."

"What?" questioned Mark, "you know this crow, I mean man?"

"My lord," the young man now bowed before Mark. "I am honoured to make your acquaintance." He held out his hand and shook Mark's with gusto, turning to Elliott and bowing again, "My Lord." Elliott shook the young man's hand and stood there looking as equally surprised as Mark.

"And you must be Jessica, never a more beautiful Watcher have I been blessed to meet."

The young man took Jess's hand and kissed it in the same way he had Roisin's. Jess too blushed at this encounter, he really was a charming young man.

"I will explain later, Mark," Roisin whispered to Mark "I think I met him in Ireland but I never knew until now."

The young man stepped forward. "Silas is in his garden, we need to wait until he leaves before it is safe to proceed. We cannot risk your quest failing before it has begun, we are all relying on your success."

"No pressure then," added Elliott.

"I will wait in the garden and when he leaves I will return for you," said the young man.

"Wait, what do we call you?" asked Roisin.

"Why, Crow of course, have you ever called me by anything else," smiled the young man in reply.

With that there was a flurry of feathers and the crow flew down the tunnel and out of the opening.

"Well I guess we just wait here then," replied Mark. The group all sat on the floor in the tunnel and waited.

"I'm actually starving now we have a moment to think," said Elliott.

"Me too" replied Jess and Roisin in unison.

The group was quiet until Mark jumped up. "What is it, Mark?" asked Jess.

"Good old Nanny," laughed Mark, the others looked puzzled, that was until he pulled a handful of wagon wheels out of his bag pack.

"Enjoy. I have a feeling this will be the last quiet moment we get for a while, once we leave this tunnel, our *quest* as Crow called it, begins."

Chapter Nineteen
Friends from the past

Moments seemed like hours as they sat in the dark, dank, dungeon like tunnel; there was a sense of anticipation and excitement.

The last week had been like the pages of a story book and no one sat in this dismal place was the same person they had been a week ago.

Jess looked around at her niece and nephews. She smiled to herself as they sat staring into the dark, listening for the crow, ready, waiting and confident but not one of them looked afraid.

She had to admit she was a little afraid. She was in a strange place, in a strange time and with no gifts of her own to protect her, she knew they would let no harm come to her and she hoped that her help wouldn't be needed. Not because she was afraid to help but because if she was needed, it meant they were hurt.

The silence was almost deafening as the darkness wrapped around them like a damp, dark blanket.

"It's clear." Roisin stood up as she spoke, relieved to break the silence.

"Shouldn't we wait? Crow said he would tell us when it was clear?" asked Elliott.

"He just told me," smiled Roisin, enjoying her new power.

Before Elliott could respond Crow flew into the tunnel, with a flurry his feathers transformed into his cloak and Crow, the young man stood before them once more.

"It's clear. We need to move quickly before Silas returns, he will have his own preparations to complete before the solstice. We must get you to Lady Isabella without delay." Crow led the way towards the exit of the tunnel.

"How did you know we were here? Or that we were coming at all?" asked Elliott.

"The threads of time are already cast, my Lord, for some of us they are threads that we can travel, as you have. Follow me, I cannot take human form outside or in daylight but I will stay close. My Lady Roisin, you will need to lead the way as no one else can communicate with me in my true form."

Crow raised his arms and his cloak fluttered once more into a beautiful pair of wings as he flew into the daylight.

As they emerged from the tunnel the daylight stung their eyes and they were greeted with the most beautiful sight, a well-tended manicured garden with herb beds and exotic flowers they had never seen before. In the middle of the garden stood a beautiful apple tree, covered in blossom and fruit.

"This is Silas's garden, remember it from the book," stated Elliott

"Yes, I remember," replied Roisin. "Let's get out of here it gives me the creeps."

"Wait I need to check something." Elliott ran towards the opening of Silas's cave.

"Elliott, come back, what are you doing?" Mark shouted in a hushed tone.

"I have to check, I promised Nanny I would fix it."

Elliott ran into Silas's cave and disappeared from view.

The others held their breath in stunned silence and waited for Elliott to emerge from the cave. "I have it"

Elliott ran from the cave, his curls bouncing as he did and his smile was from ear to ear, he was clearly happy with himself. As he ran, he held the black handled cane above his head.

"What are you doing?" asked Roisin. "Silas could come back."

"If Silas doesn't have his cane, he can't hide it in the blessing tunnel. If he can't hide it, I can't find it and if I can't find it, he can't take it back so he yes he can't hit Isabella on the head with it! Boom! I fixed it."

"Hi Five!" Mark held out his hand and Elliott slapped it as he ran past.

"Come on," shouted Elliott. "What are you all standing around for? Crow's waiting."

They all followed Crow through the forest, it was thick with oak trees and wild flowers and they had to jump the occasional fallen branch. Mark stopped suddenly and looked around. "I have been here before, with Siar, we were running away from Silas."

Roisin stopped and fell to her knees, Mark ran over to her. "Roisin, are you OK?" As Mark placed his hand on her shoulder Roisin encountered her first experience of the sight.

"Roisin, Roisin." Mark shook her by the shoulders but she just stared blankly ahead as though looking at something that only she could see.

"Jess, do something, what's wrong with her?"

Before Jess could reply Roisin was starting to come around, she looked a little dazed but was otherwise back to her normal self. "Crow, he's here, he's in the forest and he knows someone else is here, and he's running towards us."

"Don't worry," Crow replied but only Roisin could hear him.

"Keep running and head towards the smoke, that's the chimney at Lady Isabella's. I will fly back and see if I can see where he is."

"Thank you." Roisin replied and then informed everyone else what Crow had said.

They all ran as though their lives depended on it, heading towards the winding smoke they could see through the trees.

"What just happened?" Mark called to his sister as they sprinted through the forest.

"I'm not sure, it was like staring into the flames at Isabella's. I could see things happening around me but I wasn't a part of it," replied Roisin.

"Well, all the better for us, that's another power to add to your list," shouted Elliott running alongside.

"Hey can't Mark and Jess *blur* us to Isabella's?"

"Great idea!" shouted Mark. "Come on, Jess, let's try, you grab Roisin's hand and I will grab Elliott."

Mark and Jess reached out for Elliott and Roisin, the moment their hands connected, they moved at the speed of light through the forest and arrived at the front gate of Widdershins.

"That was amazing!" beamed Elliott.

"I don't know about that, I need to get my bearings I feel a little light headed," said Roisin. They stood at the gateway to Widdershins, at the bottom of the path they had only walked down a few hours before. It looked exactly the same, not similar, not almost the same, identical. The same flower pot stood outside the door with the same herbs flowering in it. The same roses climbed the trellis over the entrance. It was as though they had stepped back in time, or forward as the case may be.

Crow flew towards the front door and as he did it opened. He flew into the kitchen and with a flurry of feathers and cloth, Crow transformed once more before their eyes. "Lady Isabella," Crow began. "They have arrived."

With that announcement, he bowed out of the way with a sweep of his cloak to reveal Roisin, Mark, Elliott and Jess standing sheepishly at the door.

"Don't just stand there, we have been expecting you, please take a seat. We are expecting more guests yet, I believe you may have a note for me?"

"But how...?" Roisin started to ask but then stopped herself. If the last few weeks had taught her anything it was not to be surprised by anything any more, especially if Isabella was involved.

Roisin passed the brown folded paper to Isabella. Just as the group sat down at the table the door of the farmhouse opened fully with a gust of fresh forest air and in walked four extremely tall gentlemen, the guardians.

Suth was the first to speak. "My Lady Isabella." He spoke as he took a seat at one of the large corner chairs of the kitchen table and smiled warmly at his host, a smile of friendship but also of worry.

"My Lord, you are welcome."

Lady Isabella waved her hand to the three remaining large corner chairs to direct the three other gentlemen to their seats; they would have to be seated as the four of them filled the small kitchen towering over the other guests.

Lady Isabella turned to face her other guests. "Now the Guardians of the Quarters are here we may begin."

As Isabella spoke the room filled with the sound of voices, the group scanned the room, they could hear a nervous chatter which now started to subside. They were not alone in the kitchen of Widdershins, neither were the guardians, in fact, it now appeared more of a gathering, a gathering of what can only be described as the most unusual collection of characters straight out of a story book. These were indeed the Forest folk.

The friends of the forest had heard the call and they knew that this night of all nights they would need to be at their best, for this was the night that darkness would come and if Silas had his way, darkness would stay.

Isabella stood quietly beside the fireplace reading the note Roisin had passed her, she then folded it neatly into her apron pocket and held up her hand to quiet to the room.

The room fell silent and all eyes were on Isabella. "We have guests at our gathering today, they have journeyed through time to be here with us. These are the next generation of Darach Nua in our time, but I am sad to say, the first in over thirteen hundred years in their own time. We have planned the veil for many months and thanks to our new friends' efforts we now know this will not work. Silas will come for the sunstone this evening and we must be ready. He knows they are here, he felt their presence in the forest.

"We must protect as they have come to protect us but rest assured, I have it on very good authority that the Darach Nua of the future are not like those of our time, they are very capable warriors and the gifts of power they have been bestowed, far outreach any we have seen before."

There was a general buzz around the kitchen as the forest folk all chattered to each other and looked and pointed at the guests. The guests who were now blushing and looking anything but warrior like sitting humbly at the table.

"We need to stay sharp," continued Isabella. "We all know, it could only take Silas to use his cane to call the Underworld and we could be defeated."

"He can't," interrupted Elliott. "He can't use his cane to call anyone, I have it," Elliott stood up and held the cane with the black poplar handle above head. The forest folk gasped in disbelief and even Isabella looked shocked. "Where did you get that from and please, don't wave it around."

Elliott addressed the room. "I took it from his cave, where we have come from. Silas has used this to hurt someone I care about very much, we must destroy it to prevent him from using it again. Mark, can you break it?"

Elliott passed the cane to Mark and just as asked Mark broke the cane in half and then half again. He then passed it back to Elliott.

Elliott stepped forward and passed the cane to Isabella. "Lady Isabella, could you make sure this is never used again?"

"It would be my pleasure, Elliott of the Darach Nua."

Isabella smiled at Elliott with such warmth he was sure she knew him in this time as well as his own.

Isabella turned back to the forest folk smiling. "Allow me to introduce our new friends, you will get to know them very well in the short time we have together. You have my word that they can be trusted and they are, after all Darach Nua, it is intrinsic in their nature to protect you so please welcome them and help them in any way we can."

Isabella turned to Elliott and held her out her hand. "This is Elliott Robb, of the great Northern Clan Robb. He has been gifted with many powers, do not let his size deceive you, for he is a mighty warrior and strategist, he has the gift of magic and can move anything by thought alone."

The forest folk applauded. Elliott blushed, a strategist he thought, he liked that, he wondered had Isabella wrote that in the note.

Isabella now turned to Mark and held out her hand. Mark stood up as requested. "This is Mark O'Neill of the great Clan O'Neill, defender of the good and protector of the people and a personal friend of Siar, our very own Guardian of the West."

You could hear the gasps of surprise at the introduction and the forest folk were impressed, clapping and cheering. Isabella looked towards Siar as she spoke and they both nodded to each other in acknowledgement.

Mark was now also blushing and sat down again beside Roisin. "Is this really happening?" he asked, "Defender of the good? me, I like it." Mark was beaming and his cheeks were flushed.

Isabella now held out her hand towards Roisin. "You are honoured to meet our very own Lady Roisin O'Neill of the great Clan O'Neill. She has the gift of sight and empathy and has read The book of Widdershins and she is skilled in communication with both man and beast."

The forest folk stood up when they heard this, no one could read the book of Widdershins, no one that is unless chosen by the guardians.

Roisin's face flushed to scarlet as she sat beside Mark. "Was she talking about me? I didn't realise they would know about the book?"

170

"Our final guest is Jessica Burgess of the house of Bourgeois. Jessica is the Watcher, she has been gifted with the powers of healing and speed and has the soul of an empath. Jessica's skills will protect us all this night, if anyone is injured, be sure to speak to Jessica before the solstice, we will need all of us to be as able bodied as possible, that is..." Isabella turned to look at Jess, "if you have no objection to healing your people here today?"

Jess repeated the words over in her head *healing your people,* she felt quite overwhelmed and yet flooded with adrenaline. "It would be my honour if I am able," smiled Jess.

"Then our introductions are complete, please sit eat and talk among yourselves for a very short while and then the preparations will be begin. Beth, can you help with the refreshments?"

Isabella turned to a very pretty dark-haired young girl sat with the forest folk. "But please don't let Lucy steal the food." Isabella smiled as she gestured to Lucy, a beautiful chocolate Labrador lay at Beth's feet.

The room was filled with a buzz and a chatter once more as various guests made their way to the group to introduce themselves. Roisin was talking to the Chief Squirreller named Paige. Paige looked around nine or ten years of age but as Roisin spoke to her she realised she was much wiser than her years. Squirrellers were very important for the forest folk, they did just as their name suggested and squirrelled away all that was needed, whether that be food supplies for the winter or weapons of a war to help the forest folk against the Dall. Paige informed Roisin that whatever they needed this night she would supply, as the squirrellers had known for two summers that something was about to happen, but they hadn't known what, to this end they had bulked out the stores with magical herbs, food supplies, bows, arrows, furs and just about anything that might be needed if dark times came.

"We will be great friends, Roisin, I can feel it in my heart. You have my trust and that of my people, you only need to ask and we will serve you." Paige took Roisin by the hand as she spoke and Roisin could feel the warmth of friendship from her.

"I know we will too," replied Roisin squeezing Paige's hand.

Roisin looked for Mark, she couldn't see him in the crowd of people chattering and milling around the room. As she turned around towards the fireplace she saw him, head and shoulders above everyone else in the room. She was sure he had grown since they had arrived through the tunnel.

She smiled and waved to attract his attention. As she did, she caught his eye and he waved and nudged Elliott who was stood beside him. Elliott waved too, he was clearly in his element, enjoying all the attention.

Roisin made her way through the crowded room and as she approached Mark and Elliott she looked up. The expression on Mark's face had changed; his face was pale and drained of colour and he was staring at something. She tried to see but she was much shorter than Mark and couldn't see past the many heads in front of her; whatever it was Elliott had just seen it and the colour drained from his face also. Mark and Elliott stood white faced and expressionless staring at something that Roisin couldn't see. She reached out and touched Mark's arm, the moment their skin connected she knew what they had seen without the need to see it with her own eyes. The horror in Mark's mind transferred to Roisin and she knew.

SILAS.

Silas stood in the doorway to the kitchen and stared, his yellow sallow skin added to the dark sunken look of his eyes, he looked truly evil.

Silas raised his arms and threw a powdery dust around the room. It sparkled as it started to settle on the forest folk. He began to speak. "Frozen in time, frozen by me. Unable to help, only to see."

He repeated the words as he walked through the crowd of people who appeared to be unable to move or speak and could only watch what was unfolding before their eyes. As Silas approached Isabella and the guardians he threw more powder, he stood in front of them smirking. "You may be stronger than the forest folk and I may only be able to hold you for a short while, but I can hold you for long enough."

The fear was clear in Isabella's eyes, she was unable to move and she looked to her left at Siar, only her eyeballs moving, her body frozen mid movement. Siar looked back at Isabella, but it was not fear in his eyes but fury. He too, was unable to move but the expression within his eyes was unmistakable, he was furious.

172

Silas poked Siar to see did he move.

"I see that look in your eyes, for once I have the upper hand, but I am wise enough not to hang around long enough for you to even try to exact your revenge, look at the five of you, Guardians, Keeper of Time, you are nothing compared to the power I will have when I take the final stone, my sun stone this solstice, the power of the Underworld will be mine and you will finally kneel to my will."

Silas turned on his heels and marched towards the fireplace.

The cousins stood motionless, only their eyes darted around the room to see what was happening, Mark caught Jess's eye and she looked horrified but she also couldn't move.

Silas stood before the three cousins smirking. He bent down beside the fireplace and retrieved the burnt black poplar handle of his cane from the grate; without standing but staying crouched down beside the fire, he looked up at the cousins and threw back his head laughing. He tapped what remained of his cane on the ground three times and stood up. "Take us down, three plus me, into the Underworld beyond the Black Sea."

Three times again he tapped his cane. Silas and the cousins vanished, they were nowhere to be seen and a cold, empty silence filled the kitchen.

Chapter Twenty
The final battle

Jess sat stunned and silent at the kitchen table. Beth brought her sweet tea to try and help her with the shock. Isabella took Jess's hand and squeezed it. "We will fix this, it is never as dark as it seems, if we unravel the threads the plan and the pattern will come to us." Isabella spoke softly to Jess.

"I came with them to help them, to heal them if they needed me, how can I help them if I don't know where they are?" Jess started to sob.

Tuath held up his hand in a gesture to interrupt. "It is not where but when. I feel their energy within me, they are within the earth in the Underworld, time does not travel along the same threads in the Underworld, but they are there I can feel their energy in the Earth. If we can locate them, we can summon them back and Silas too. We don't have long before the sun sets for the solstice. Jessica, you are their Watcher, if I can feel them you should be able to contact them. Concentrate, we will help you."

The four guardians stood up, creating a circle around Jess. "Concentrate" said Siar. "Think of their faces and their thoughts will follow." The guardians started to chant...

"Guardians of the watchtower we four, Darach Nua we are opening the door. Between the realms our powers reach, open your minds and give it speech."

As each word was spoken the guardians stamped their feet on the floor. Tuath pounded his cane on the kitchen floor in time with each word.

The momentum started to build, each syllable of each word defined, each word coincided with a mighty thud on the ground. It started to sound tribal, the chant grew in volume and ferocity, the forest folk joined in.

Jess looked around the room, she had never seen or heard anything like it. The guardians loomed over her in height and the sound they made was making every part of her body vibrate, it was as though the ground itself was humming in response. The forest folk were now in unison with the guardians and looked equally as fierce and determined. The whole kitchen was shaking from the foot stamping and the chanting that was unbearably loud. Jess started to feel light headed, the sound buzzed through her, all the words jumbling into one.

Then it stopped.

She looked around and the chanting continued in as much frenzy as before but no sound could be heard. It was as though someone had hit the mute button on the tv remote control. Then she heard it, no that was wrong, there was no sound, she felt it, it felt as though she were being drawn to a sound she couldn't hear. She tried to focus, to get clarity in her mind.

"Jess."

There it was, she heard it, she definitely heard it. Jess squinted her eyes in a bid to hear clearly.

"Jess, can you hear me?"

It was Roisin's voice, it was just as clear as though she were stood beside her. "I can hear you," shouted Jess.

"Jess, can you hear me?" Roisin's voice repeated the question as though no answer had been given.

"I'm here, Roisin, I can hear you," shouted Jess desperately.

"Jess, if you can hear me, talk to me with your mind, talk to me in your thoughts, are you there, Jess?"

Jess stopped for a moment, Roisin couldn't hear her speak. She wasn't here, whatever the guardians were doing it had opened a doorway to wherever they were and Jess could hear Roisin in her head, not in the room. Jess realised it would be the same for Roisin. She placed her hands to her temples as Elliott had done earlier and focused her mind, she was after all the Watcher. If anyone could reach them, surely the Watcher could.

"Roisin, I'm here, where are you? Are you all together? Are you hurt?"

"Jess, it's so good to hear your voice. I think we are in the Underworld, in Silas's cave. I recognise it from reading Widdershins. We are all together, we are OK but we are trapped, we can't leave the cave, it's as though there is a shield around it. We are trapped in a circle by, I'm not sure, a sort of invisible prism of energy. Mark's asleep and he's been asleep since we got here I'm worried."

"Don't be worried, Roisin, we are here and the guardians are going to help, try to wake Mark, why is he asleep?"

"I'm trying but he won't wake up and he's so big now I can't move him, Jess! He must have banged his head, there is blood on his hair, Jess, what do I do?"

Before Roisin had finished speaking Jess was beside her, in the cave, her hands checking through Mark's hair, looking for his wound.

"Jess, how did you?" Roisin started to ask.

"Jess, it's so good to see you, but how?" Elliott stated giving Jess a huge hug.

"I don't know, I just felt that Mark needed me and then I was here."

Jess placed her hands where the blood was seeping out, it was a cut about five centimetres long. It looked as though however they landed in this cave Mark had hit his head on a jagged rock.

Jess held her hand over the cut and felt the heat radiate from her own hands, then the heat stopped. When she removed her hands, Mark began to stir.

"Jess, you must go back, they are calling you."

"Who is? I only just arrived"

"Siar is calling you, you are on another plane here and your body is back there. If you leave it for too long you can't return to your body and you will be trapped here. Quickly go back, speak to Isabella, there must be something they can do to get us out."

Roisin and Elliott both hugged Jess.

"Speak to Isabella and the guardians, we aren't going anywhere in a hurry, they will know what to do," said Elliott.

Jess opened her eyes and she was laying on the kitchen floor again. Isabella held out her hand to help Jess to her feet.

"You travelled the plain to the Underworld, that is hard on the mind and the body. No Watcher has been capable of such feats before, come sit, we have a plan."

The four guardians, Isabella, the leaders of the forest folk and Jess, all gathered around the kitchen table, it was like a meeting of a war counsel.

Siar spoke on behalf of the guardians. Silas had gone too far this time, not only had he yet again travelled to the Underworld which was forbidden, he had spirited away the Darach Nua against their will. He had trapped them in the Underworld in a bid to stop them from calling an end to his plans for the Sun stone.

Isabella explained that they had been planning for many months to cast a veil that would stop Silas from taking the stone but she now knew, from the note that Roisin had given her that this was no longer an option. They needed to get the stone back to the tunnel so that the Darach Nua could take it with them to the future, but before they could do this, they needed to stop Silas once and for all. This would not be easy given that he was now in the Underworld and he had taken the Darach Nua with him and held them prisoner in his cave.

"Silas thinks he is wise, this has always been his problem, he doesn't doubt his own wisdom," Siar explained.

"He has taken himself to the Underworld in a bid to hide, but hide from who? The Underworld is a dark, cold and lonely place, but the only beings that are there are the ones that we have banished from here. There may be no sunlight and no moon to bring warmth and guidance but it is still the earth, it is still ruled by the elements, as are all things."

"I don't understand," said Jess looking confused.

"We will summon Silas to his own cave, as above so below," said Siar and he got up and left Widdershins. The other guardians got up and filed out behind him.

"Isabella, I don't understand, what's going on?" asked Jess.

"It is better you don't know the details, but trust me, we will not make the same error twice. Does Elliott have the amber necklace on him?"

"Yes, he hasn't taken it off since he found it, but why?"

Jess got up as she spoke and followed Isabella across the kitchen. "He will need it this night, sit by the fire and watch the flames. You need to contact Roisin, tell her we are coming for them. They will know when the times right and when it is, Mark needs to deosil the three of them to the blessing passage."

"Deosil?" Jessica started to ask but then remembered her

conversation with Sean. "Ahh you mean blur."

Isabella looked at Roisin clearly confused, "Blur?" "Don't worry, I know what we both mean," smiled Jess.

Jess did as she was instructed, she cleared her mind and stared into the flames. She found it much easier the second time to find Roisin's voice in the distance.

She explained to Roisin exactly as Isabella had instructed and added that Mark needed to blur the three of them to the blessing passage as soon as they were given the signal; unfortunately, just now, no one knew exactly what that signal would be or how the guardians intended on getting them from the Underworld.

Isabella was in the far corner of the kitchen giving very precise instructions to Paige and Beth. Paige was to lead the squireller's and Beth was to help. They were to take everything the squireller's had saved that could emit light. Isabella wanted a clear well-lit pathway through the forest from Silas's garden down to the blessing passage at Goderich Brook. They must take Lucy with them so she could warn them if Silas returned. Isabella asked that all the squierreller's help and it was imperative that the pathway was lit before the sun set as they were running out of time.

"Elliott, I hear someone approaching," Roisin whispered to Elliott.

"Get Mark back onto his feet, quickly, it might be Silas."

Roisin and Elliott both grabbed one of Mark's arms to try and stand him up. Mark sat up straight away as though woken from a deep sleep. "What are you doing? I can stand up on my own."

"Mark, you hurt your head when we got here, Jess came and fixed it and you have been sleeping. I think I heard someone outside the cave and I was afraid." Roisin squeezed Mark's hand as she spoke.

"Little big sister, don't be afraid. I won't let anyone or anything hurt you, either of you." Mark stood up and moved in front of Roisin and Elliott. As he did two figures appeared at the gateway to the cave.

"You are the Darach Nua we have heard tell of," spoke the boy. "You are very young in years, how weak the Darach Nua must be in the future."

Mark stepped forward. "Don't come any closer or you will find out just how weak we are."

"Tell me your name," said the boy to Mark.

Mark was about to reply when Elliott stepped forward. "Tell them nothing, cousin, to give them our names would give them power over us, remember when Silas came here first."

"I see you have learned lessons from the past, that won't help you now. Your powers are useless here." As the boy spoke he and his sister walked towards the edge of the circle the cousins were trapped within. Behind them followed a crowd of people and they did not look like they wanted to make friends.

"Roisin, Elliott, get behind me." Mark stood in front of Roisin and Elliott. "Stay back or I won't be responsible for what happens to you!"

Mark spoke confidently and without fear to the crowd now gathering around the circle, they were inching forward and each time they took a step the circle shrank a little smaller.

"Cerberus, heel." The boy called Cerberus to his side. "Fetch."

The words echoed in the air as the boy commanded the three headed dog to *fetch,* the cousins.

Cerberus entered the circle and walked slowly towards them, all three heads lowered, tails hissing and drool dripping from its mouths.

Mark rushed forward and jumped onto Cerberus as though he was jumping onto the back of a horse. He wrestled the large hound to the ground and a vicious scrap ensued, dust filled the circle and it was unclear who was winning.

"Stop, you will get hurt," shouted Roisin in tears.

"Cousin, grab his tails, I have control of his heads," Mark shouted from somewhere within the dust cloud.

Elliott didn't hesitate for a moment on hearing Mark's request and dove into the middle of the foray.

"Tie them together."

Elliott followed Mark's instructions.

The crowd around the circle were shouting and jeering with delight at the gladiatorial scene before them.

The dust started to settle and it was clear who had lost in this battle. Cerberus lay unconscious on the ground with his three heads limp and lifeless. The tails still hissed but they were tightly bound and unable to move.

Mark and Elliott dusted themselves off and stepped back towards Roisin. "If anyone else tries anything, you will get the same treatment," Mark advised. The boy and the girl looked furious.

"Enough," shouted the boy. "It is time to feast, they are yours to enjoy!" As the boy spoke he lifted his arms and signalled to the now rowdy crowd that was surrounding the circle. "Feast on the Darach Nua!" He dropped his arms to signal to the crowd and they started to move forward to enjoy the feast.

As the sun started to set Isabella, Crow and Jess made their way to Silas cave. It was easy to find as Paige and Beth had completed their task admirably, the pathway was well lit and easy to follow. When they reached Silas's cave the guardians were there waiting.

"I don't understand, Isabella, what is happening?"

"Basic laws of nature, my dear, as above so below, the guardians are going to reverse Silas's cave, so the Underworld is above and his cave is below. The moment he realises what is happening he will come back and that I hope, is where we trap him, locking him inside the earth, or at least the symbol of the earth. Let's hope Elliott is wearing the amulet that I gave to Silas, that Tuath gave to Elliott. Once he's trapped, the four of you will need to deosil to the blessing passage and take the stone back through the corridor and through the gateway in time."

Jess stood with Isabella at the entrance to the cave, the forest folk filled the garden. Jess closed her eyes tightly and pictured Roisin's face, "We are coming for you," she whispered.

"Hurry, we are not alone and they intend to feast on us!" Roisin's voice whispered back in Jess's mind.

"Quickly," called Jess. "They are not alone and they are in real danger."

The guardians took position in the cave, each at their own compass point. Isabella walked around them sprinkling salt.

She stood in the centre of the circle and called each quarter by name, as she did the air was filled with the raw elemental power.

Lightning cracked overhead, the very earth beneath their feet began to shake, the wind whipped up into a frenzy and the rains came. It was a storm to rival all storms and it swirled around them, battering them with rain, and almost blowing them to the ground with the power of the wind.

Siar held up his cane, as did Suth, Tuath and Ost, lightning struck their canes and the chanting began.

"Guardians of the watchtower we four, Darach Nua we are opening the door. As above, so below the threefold law its powers will show. As is above, so below. As above, so below."

The forest folk now joined in with the chanting, shouting at the top of their voices through the howling wind and rain. "As above, so below. As above so below."

The sound of the storm was deafening, the earth rumbled but it was different, the earth itself was moving, the ground in the centre of the cave cracked and through the gap you could see a prism rising up. As more of the prism became visible, you could see the cousins stood in the centre, pushing back the sides of the circle. There were arms grabbing for them and a horrendous roar of the unyielding crowd around them.

Jess looked on in horror, the crowd seemed to reach through the sides of the circle and tear at their clothes and skin.

"Quickly, they don't have much time!" she shouted to the guardians.

The air was heavy with electric from the storm and the drumbeat that seemed to accompany the chanting. As the ground settled and the prism burst through the earth leaving the hungry crowd below the chanting stopped but the storm didn't subside. The chanting started again, this time it was Tuath leading the chant.

"Silas," and he stamped his foot.

"Silas," the other guardians joined in and stamped their feet.

"Silas," the forest folk joined in stamping their feet and banging on anything they had to hand.

The ground within the prism started to shake and a crack appeared in the ground.

Jess could not believe her eyes as she looked on and from the crack within the ground, within the prism, Silas was rising.

"Wait!" shouted Jess. "What are you doing? He will be in there with them," The chanting stopped and Silas was now inside the prism with the cousins. Tuath shouted to Elliott. "Elliott, your amulet, put Silas in your amulet."

Elliott looked at him dumbstruck, he looked at Silas and then at the amulet. He turned to Roisin and Mark in disbelief. "He's never gonna fit in there!"

"Use your mind, picture him inside it," shouted Isabella. "The guardians will help you."

Elliott looked around again, hoping that someone would agree with how crazy this sounded, but no, everyone was watching and waiting.

"Flippen 'eck!" he shouted and jumped into fighting stance. He placed his hands on his temples and screwed up his eyes as he stared intently at Silas. Nothing happened.

Silas rushed towards the cousins and Mark wrestled him to the floor. "Keep your hands where I can see them this time," Mark shouted at Silas.

Elliott jumped up and changed fighting stance and resumed his stare. Silas tried to run to escape and to get to the cousins but he was powerless against Mark's strength. Then Silas started to rise up. Mark jumped up quickly and stepped back.

"What's happening?" shouted Roisin.

"It's Elliott, he's controlling Silas," Mark replied as stunned as his sister by what was happening before his eyes.

Elliott continued concentrating on Silas as Silas flailed around trying to regain control of his body. "It's not working I'm not strong enough."

Mark stepped forward and put his hand on Elliott's shoulder. "Roisin, we are at our strongest when we work together, remember Isabella told us." Roisin ran over to Elliott and placed her hand on his shoulder.

"Come on, picture him in my amulet," shouted Elliott.

The cousins all stared at Silas, willing him into the amulet.

The guardians and the forest folk continued to chant. There was a huge crack of lightning, the storm stopped and there was an eerie silence. The prism was gone and the cousins were stood in the cave with the guardians and there was no sign of Silas.

"The amulet, Elliott, is he in the amulet?" Roisin asked, her voice high pitched with adrenaline and urgency.

"I can't see him?" Elliott replied, turning the amulet over in his hand. "But look!" He held up the amber amulet to show his cousins. It was still the same beautiful amber coloured stone on one side, but the reverse was now the smooth black stone, as it had been in the vision in the fire at Isabella's when Silas had worn it.

"You don't have much time," said Crow. "You need to return before the new day begins."

Crow walked over to Roisin and gave her a huge hug, wrapping his cloak around her as he did. "I'm happier than you can ever know now that you are safe," he said warmly.

Roisin responded with the same warmth but she could not help but notice that the soft velvety cloak tickled her skin like feathers.

"The vials," shouted Elliott. "Save some for Jess."

Jess looked up as he said this, she was busy hugging Mark and Roisin.

"Thank you, Elliott, one thing is for sure I do not want to be left behind and besides, you need me to blur." She hugged Elliott a little too enthusiastically almost squeezing his breath from his body. "I was so worried about you."

"Please hurry, you have no time for chatter," Isabella insisted.

Roisin, Mark, Elliott and Jess each drank their share of the vials with the label 2018. They all joined hands and nodded in agreement.

"Let's do this," they said in unison.

Mark and Jess led the way at the speed of light, taking Elliott and Roisin with them, the blessing passage was easy to find thanks to Beth and Paige's well-lit pathway. They walked down the steps into the passage which was far more beautiful and sculpted now than it was in their time and there it was, shining like a beacon just under the water in Goderich brook. Mark tried to lift it but it would not budge, it was stuck in the suction of the mud.

"Stand back," said Elliott. "I will release it and you can try to carry it, Mark, I will take some of the weight as you do."

"Sounds like a plan to me." Mark stood there in readiness waiting for the stone.

Elliott assumed his stance, fingers on temples and gave the sun stone his undivided attention. You could hear the sound of the mud releasing its grip on the stone, a wet, squelching, suction sound as it rose into the air.

"Listen," said Roisin.

"What is it?" asked Jess.

"The dawn chorus is about to start, I feel the birds waking up."

Roisin replied.

"Roisin, grab a hold of Jess, Elliott stick with me and the stone, follow the lights back to the cave and head straight through the tunnel and up the steps. We have no time to waste, don't stop until you are in Nanny's kitchen. Let's go."

The four of them all followed Mark's instructions, through the forest, back into the dark cold tunnel, up the stairs.

"My squirrels!"

Nanny's voice was the first thing they heard as they burst through the gateway into her kitchen. The second thing they noticed was the bright light streaming in through the window.

The third thing they noticed, was Isabella collapsing onto the floor.

Chapter Twenty-One
Your adventures have only just begun

For what should have been a time for celebration, the mood in Isabella's kitchen was very sombre.

Isabella was sat in her armchair in front of the fire with her large patchwork blanket draped over her knees. Everyone else was gathered around on various chairs. Isabella didn't look unwell but she did look old, understandably, given all that they now knew.

"I have asked you all to gather around as I have an announcement. I don't want to see all these sad faces, this is not a day of sadness but of celebration. I have waited a lifetime and then a lifetime more for this day.

"My work is now complete and I can move on knowing that the Darach Nua is strong and able to restore the natural balance to the world. It will take time and you cannot do it alone. But you are not alone. Sean and Rowan will be here and whilst they have no powers, they have a world of knowledge of the old ways and will always give you any guidance you need.

"You have Jess, who has proven that she is not only a Watcher but *the* Watcher. I have never seen one so gifted in all my years. You have each other and again you have proven that you are stronger, wiser and more gifted than any Darach Nua that came before you. Your hearts are pure and you will only grow wiser and stronger in time.

"Time, this brings me nicely to my final point. I have been the Keeper of Time for so long I can barely remember when my time began. I could not pass on the honour, as there was no way that I could be sure that time would be kept and the balance restored. Not until now."

The cousins looked at each other in horror. "Isabella," Roisin muttered, her eyes wet with tears. "You can't leave us, we need you, who will guide and protect us?"

"The one person that I know would protect you with her life, your nanny."

A gasp went around the room. Nanny stood open-mouthed looking at Isabella. "Isabella, I'm truly honoured that you would think so highly of me, but what about you? I can't follow in your footsteps, no one can, where will you go?" Nanny asked, clearly shocked by Isabella's announcement.

"I have the rest of the summer to spend with you, to teach you all I can, but then I will be gone and you will all need to fulfil your destiny without me. The Darach Nua, The Watcher and of course, the Keeper of Time. Your destiny awaits you."

"You can't!" shouted Elliott. "You can't just give up and die!"

"Hold on just one minute, Elliott Robb." Isabella spoke quite sternly to Elliott and he stopped in his tracks to listen.

"No one mentioned anything about dying, I want to go back, I want to go home and live my life with my children as I should have done centuries ago, if I hadn't been waiting for Silas, and well I suppose, waiting for you."

"What?" asked Elliott, now sounding more shocked than angry. "You can do that? You can go back? I thought when we went back you said you couldn't as it would create a loop?"

"That is what I said, and it will create a loop, but as the Keeper of Time I can only create one loop, and if it is OK with you, Elliott, I would like it to be in a time that has no veil and no Silas."

"Elliott." Roisin scolded him and gave him the eyes that meant stop talking and stop talking now.

Elliott gave Roisin the eyes right back, he hadn't finished yet. "Does that mean we can visit, through the gateway, or that you can visit us? And well, what about past Isabella? Will she? Well I mean you, not mind there being two of you?"

"Elliott, you are asking a lot of questions of Isabella, maybe you should let her rest." Nanny spoke gently but also gave Elliott the eyes.

"It's fine," replied Isabella. "Yes it does mean we can travel through the gateway, but not all the time, there must be a good reason, and as for past me, of course I won't mind, we will be one but with all our knowledge and memories combined."

"Mother." Everyone looked around as Rowan spoke. "I want to go too, I want the chance to live and laugh and love. We missed so much because of Silas and the veil, I know we won't be Darach Nua any more, but I would like to be Rowan, in my own home, my own time, with you."

"Me too." Sean stepped forward.

"Can we all go, the three of us and be a family again?"

You could see the tears start to prick Isabella's eyes. She held out her arms to her children who instantly went to her and embraced her. "My children, of course you can, there is nothing that would make me happier." Even Elliott smiled at the scene before him.

"Isabella?" Isabella looked up from her embrace. "What happens now? Do we keep our powers? Now that we have fixed everything, saved the sun stone, captured Silas and you are going home?"

Isabella looked at Sean and Rowan and they all started to laugh. "What's so funny?" asked Mark.

"Elliott said it but I was thinking it too."

"Everyone was thinking it," smiled Roisin knowingly.

Isabella clapped her hands together, still chuckling to herself, "Fixed everything? Why you have only just begun. You have indeed captured Silas for the future, but there are places in the past that he remains. The sunstone for Widdershins is safe and secure, but it is only one, one of six.

"The balance will not be restored, not until they are all returned and magic is free to all who believe. Remember I told you of the Dall, the non-believers who couldn't see the beauty in nature's magic because of the lies of non-believers and because it had been so long from their lives? The Dall are everywhere, I hope one day with your help they will see the truth again."

Isabella looked around the room smiling. "Your adventures have only just begun."